LightLand

SCHOLASTIC INC.

NEW YORK TORONTO LONDON AUCKLAND SYDNEY
MEXICO CITY NEW DELHI HONG KONG BUENOS AIRES

Sand

H. L. McCutchen

ISBN 0-439-39566-6

12 11 10 9 8 7 6 5 4 3 2   4 5 6 7 8 9/0

Printed in the U.S.A.   40

First paperback printing, August 2004

Original hardcover edition designed
by Elizabeth B. Parisi, published by Orchard Books,
an imprint of Scholastic Inc.,
November 2002.

JULIA MARIE KANNAM AND CATHERINE CLARA KANNAM

I WROTE THIS STORY FOR YOU.

CONTENTS

PROLOGUE

Lottie Cook's mother died the same minute that Lottie was born. Her father said she came into this world with her eyes wide open, and that may be the reason why her earliest memories were amazingly clear. She remembered the cold metal of the hospital crib and the flat, tinny taste of powdered baby formula. She did! She remembered her father's long, lonely hands holding her, carrying her home from the hospital by himself. She remembered his wide, flat smile the first time she ever saw it.

Remembering was Lottie's avocation. She had started by collecting stories about the mother that she never knew. Even when she was a tiny child, her father depended on her to gather the memories, keep them safe, and share them. When she was three, four years old, she was a miniature storyteller telling tiny, miniature stories. As she grew, so did her stories.

The first magic thing happened to Lottie when she turned eleven years old. That was the year that her great adventures began. But to fully understand these things, it's best to go backward a bit, to a rainy summer morning years earlier, when six-year-old Lottie was banging on a locked door.

CHAPTER ONE

The StoryBox

Lottie and her father lived alone in a strange little house in the middle of an Iowa cornfield. This particular stormy morning, six-year-old Lottie was locked out of her father's Building Room. It was a week before the first day of first grade. She was peeking through the gaping crack at the bottom of the crooked, homemade door when she heard the sound of shuffling feet. She didn't have to look up; she knew that shuffle by heart.

"Lewis, take a look," Lottie whispered.

"What is he doing this time?"

"I don't know. All I can see is his feet."

Six-year-old Lewis Weaver was Lottie's best friend. Lottie was Lewis's *only* friend. No one else knew how to be friends with Lewis because he wouldn't talk to them. At all. He hadn't uttered a word until he was three years old, and then when he did, it was exclusively to Lottie. This was the first thing to know about him: The only person in the entire world that he talked to was Lottie. This irritated his mother beyond description. No matter how Mrs. Weaver fussed and fumed Lewis would only nod, shrug, shake his head, and talk to Lottie when no one else could hear.

Mrs. Weaver tied a little notebook to Lewis every morning, with the idea that he would at least communicate by writing and drawing. And every evening she fussed when his notebook was only filled with strange symbols and squiggles that communicated precious little. Grown-ups in town felt certain that all this would change in just a few days when Lewis was required by law to start first grade and Things Would Be Expected Of Him.

Lewis tried to pry open the Building Room door for a peek, but it was bolted tight. He rattled the doorknob.

"Keep out!" Lottie's father bellowed through the locked door. "It's not finished! It's a present for your first day of school!"

Lottie calmly shook her head. "I'm not going to school," she said evenly to Lewis.

Kindergarten was optional in Oxford, Iowa, and so Lottie and Lewis had opted out last year. They were both plenty smart, and the town kindergarten, run by Miss Connie in her ranch house behind the post office, seemed like a colossal waste of time. Miss Connie taught advanced classes such as "Sharing: It's Not Always Your Turn" and "Glue: Not for Eating." Last year, Lottie and Lewis, who could read when they were three and write when they were four, had written and illustrated an essay outlining why they didn't need to go to kindergarten. Without consulting their parents, they had submitted the essay directly to Miss Connie. Miss Connie, embarrassed and offended, phoned their parents to say that the kindergarten class was full.

The same approach had not worked regarding first grade, but they hadn't given up yet. "I'm not going to school," Lottie repeated to the locked door. "Ever."

"Oh yes you are," her father barked back definitively.

"My mother says school is wonderful," Lewis said without conviction. Lottie and Lewis looked at each other and then burst out laughing. Nearly everything that Mrs. Weaver said made them laugh. She was always wrong.

Lewis's father had disappeared when Lewis was three. Mr. Weaver had been a brilliant scientist. No one ever spoke about him anymore, and Lewis and Lottie had the distinct feeling that everyone was afraid to even mention him. When he vanished Mrs. Weaver simply acted as though he had never existed.

Mrs. Weaver was an unpleasant woman who wore a

perpetual pucker, as though she were sucking lemons dry, Lottie said. Her brow was always furrowed. Her fists were always clenched. It was a shame.

But at least they had Lottie's father, who loved them both. Eldon Cook was a shadowy man with the longest fingers you ever saw. He was somewhat somber to the rest of the world, but when he looked at Lottie his smile could light up a room. He loved her plain brown hair. He loved the seven freckles on the bridge of her nose. He loved the deep well he fell into when he looked at her hazel eyes. And he loved the way those eyes seemed to change color with the weather. He had one treasure in this world and it was Lottie.

Late that evening, after Lewis and Lottie had made their own supper (corn bread, corn mash, and leftover Iowa cutcorn), and after Lewis had been dragged home through the rain, Lottie heard the Building Room lock turning. At last, Mr. Cook emerged with something under his arm.

It was wrapped in an old quilt, but it looked to be almost the size of a shoe box. "Ready?" he asked. She nodded, and he let her unfold the quilt.

It was, well, a shoe box. A wooden shoe box with a wooden lid that fit neatly on top. It was cherry wood, and Lottie instantly worried that he had cut down the old cherry tree by the back door. It was polished a deep, shiny, black cherry color.

"You have the best memory of anybody I've met, Lottie. You remember big things and little things and things that never even happened. There is room in that pointy head of yours to soak up everything that goes on around you. But school *is* coming."

Lottie rolled her eyes as if to say, *We'll see about that,* while Mr. Cook opened the box. The inside was brighter cherry and almost seemed to glow in the darkening room.

"At school," her father continued, "there'll be other things to remember, crowding your brain. Like five plus eight. And how to spell *Arkansas.*"

"Five plus eight equals thirteen," said Lottie.

Mr. Cook laughed and messed up her hair.

"*A-r-k-a-n-s-a-s,*" Lottie spelled.

"I know you already know everything, but you still have to go to school. So . . ." — he smiled, pleased with himself — "that's why you'll need this."

Lottie just stared.

"It's a StoryBox," her father continued. "In this box, you keep little bits and pieces of every story you need to remember. That way, when your head fills with school facts you won't run out of room and forget the truly important things." He kissed the top of her head and pressed the box into her arms.

Lottie held the smooth box, and it felt warm in her hands. "Did you cut down my cherry tree?"

"Well, now, Lottie . . . Yes and no."

Lottie bit her lip and twisted her hands and walked to the kitchen window. She pushed it open and leaned out into the storm. There, through the streaming rain, she could see — nothing. Where her favorite tree should have been was a bare patch in the yard.

"It was hit by lightning last night," her father said quietly. "The tree wouldn't have survived. But you can have the box to keep forever."

Lottie wasn't pleased. She told a story quickly. "I remember," she began quietly, "I remember . . . that tree grew before I was born when Mama spit a cherry seed from the kitchen window, and she sang to that tree every morning while she waited for her tea water to boil. And when she was gone and I was a baby, I slept on my back under cherry flowers and I could still hear her singing. . . ."

Her father was smiling quietly at her, waiting.

"We could have tried to save my tree," she said.

"I don't think it would have made it."

"But it might have."

How could she accept a gift that had taken her memory

tree away? The more she thought about it, the more furious she became with her father. "This box is very small," she said coldly. "It won't hold much."

Thunder rumbled through the cornfields outside. The box seemed to shimmer when the lightning flashed and the thunder boomed closer to home. Mr. Cook's wide, flat smile spread until he was grinning ear to ear. "I already thought of that. Just give it a try."

But Lottie didn't.

A few days later it was time for school to start. Lottie was in a terrible mood. She hadn't forgiven her father for cutting down her tree, and now he was making her go to school! She snubbed the new, yellow-checkered dress he had purchased especially for her. At five minutes to eight, she still sat at the breakfast table in her blue flannel pajamas and purple slippers.

"I hope you don't think you're wearing pajamas to school?" her father asked nervously.

"This way I can pretend that it's all a dream," Lottie mumbled to her bowl of cornflakes. Then she looked up and gave her father an icy glare. "Besides, if you make me wear anything else, I'll just take it off when I get there. Make me get dressed and I'll go naked instead. You know I would."

He knew she would. So Lottie Cook went to school in

her pajamas. Every day. She honestly didn't give a hoot what anyone else thought.

Lottie was so put out with her father for making her go to school that she sulked for the better part of *five years* and kept wearing pajamas. She wasn't teased as much as you might have guessed. What was the fun in teasing a person who just didn't care? So Lottie wore pajamas for all of first and then second grade. Sure, a few people pointed when she still wore them for third grade, fourth grade. By fifth grade it was old news.

When sixth grade rolled around, Lottie studied the Sears catalog for new thicker, fleecy pajama outfits. "The problem is walking to school in the winter," she told Lewis. "The wind cuts right through flannel."

Lottie and Lewis walked to school together four mornings a week. On Fridays Lewis was driven directly to a speech therapist in Cedar Rapids in hopes that he would learn how to talk to somebody besides Lottie.

"What do you do in speech class, Lew?" Lottie wanted to know. "You don't talk to him, do you?"

Lewis recoiled at the thought. "Of course not. I listen to him *ee-nun-see-ate* for a while. Then while he talks on and on, I go to sleep and I sleep all the way through." They laughed.

Lewis slept with his eyes open. Not catnapping, not day-dreaming. Full-out sleeping. And if you didn't know this secret — only Lottie and Mrs. Weaver knew — you would have *no idea*. While Lewis slept his thick eyelashes blinked and his dark brown eyes gazed as usual. The only thing different was that his head would tilt slightly downward and his mouth sort of relaxed. He never had dreams and he could wake up instantly when he needed to. If he responded a little slowly sometimes, people thought it was just because he was, well, a little slow.

Lottie had tried to teach Lewis how to sleep with his eyes closed, but it didn't take. Even at night, this was how Lewis slept. When he slept at night.

For the most part, however, Lewis slept through the day. He slept through school and no one noticed. Teachers never called on Lewis, since he wouldn't speak anyway. Lottie would poke him when it was time to move for lunch or a fire drill or something. He slept through church, through car rides, bus trips, and piano lessons. The other incredible thing was that Lewis seemed to absorb what was going on around him while he slept. He could still perform on recital day, never missed his bus stop, and his grades — while not spectacular — were officially Good Enough.

At night he puttered quietly around his house and some-times slipped into town if there was enough moonlight. "Just looking at things," he said. Lewis didn't really *like* the dark. It made him nervous. But when nights were clear and bright, he would venture out. Lewis's pale skin had a soft kind of light to it, which Lottie thought had to be from the moon.

This was one of the things Lottie liked best about Lewis, this mystery. Was he awake or asleep?

Lottie and Lewis both turned eleven over the summer. They always had a small party together during August. As usual, the guests included Lewis's mean-spirited cousin, James Ray from Cedar Rapids, and little Cindy Arnold from down the road. Summer birthdays were a bit of a nonevent. Most kids their age were either at summer camp, on family vacations, or too busy working the farms to help celebrate.

The few occasions when their parents got together were sources of great amusement for Lewis and Lottie. The two adults were so different that it was funny just watching them sit awkwardly next to each other on the picnic bench, trying to pretend that they enjoyed each other's company.

Mr. Cook, who was not a timid man, would ask timidly, "Had a nice summer?"

"Not especially, why do you want to know?" Mrs. Weaver would answer suspiciously. And then she'd remember her manners and smile a thin, strained smile.

Sometimes, when they wanted a good belly laugh, Lewis

and Lottie pretended that Mrs. Weaver was going to marry Mr. Cook. "And on their wedding day," Lottie would say, "opposites around the world will unite in peace, harmony, and love."

"Good and evil, day and night," said Lewis. "Perfect."

"Whipped cream and tuna fish," said Lottie. "Delicious."

For their party all Lewis and Lottie cared about was that Mrs. Weaver baked one of her incredible birthday cakes, which grew by another layer each and every year. (This year, it was eleven thin, moist layers of devil's food. Baking cakes was one thing that Mrs. Weaver did better than just about anybody. But when you said how good the cake was, she'd only scowl and tell you what was wrong with the recipe and say something like "I'll never be foolish enough to bake *that* again, let me tell you. Cost me a fortune in eggs.")

There were twenty-two candles on the massive cake this year. (They each insisted on having their own set.) It looked like a bonfire. Last year, at a mere twenty candles, it had taken them several tries to get all the flames out. So to tackle twenty-two, Lewis and Lottie took huge breaths and prepared to blow when — from out of nowhere — a narrow gust of wind whistled through the yard and snuffed out every single one. Everyone else thought Lottie and Lewis had blown them out and clapped. Mrs. Weaver starting slicing thick slabs of cake.

"Did you see that?" Lottie whispered to Lewis.

Lewis nodded, frowning.

"That's an omen, Lewis," Lottie said with a grin, biting into her cake. "Eleven is going to be a very interesting year."

Lewis looked doubtful.

"Really, Lew. School starts in two weeks, and they still haven't found anyone to teach in Miss O'Neal's place. Maybe this means they'll skip us ahead to seventh grade."

They both knew that was too good to be true. They'd hire someone to teach sixth grade, all right. And at this late date, they might scrounge up someone truly horrible. Lewis worried about it.

Lottie licked the last bit of Crisco frosting off her plate and chuckled at Lewis's troubled expression. "I've got a feeling," she insisted with a chocolatey grin. "That gust of wind was a good sign."

On September first they chatted as they walked the twenty minutes to school. Lottie felt fantastic in her new, aqua blue, fleecy Polartec pajama ensemble. Lewis looked stressed; his socks didn't match, and his crewneck was inside out. His curly dark brown hair stuck out more than usual. Even as they disappeared into the cornfield, he kept jerking his head around; he didn't want to be heard talking. But since most of their walk was through the fields on the outskirts of town, they almost never saw anyone else.

They always took the shortcut through the field. It's tricky, finding your way through tall corn rows. Unless you have an exceptional sense of direction and really know what you're doing, you can become completely disoriented and be lost for hours. It's like a thick green maze. Of course, Lottie and Lewis had done it all their lives. They loved the quiet rustling of the corn. They always sighed when they emerged from the field and had to walk along the dusty main road to town. Coming out of the corn that day, Lewis was still fretting loudly nonstop.

"I'm telling you, Lottie, new teachers make me nervous. She doesn't *know* us. She'll ask questions. She'll expect me to talk. She'll want you to wear real clothes. It can't be good."

"Ohh, come on, Lew, how do you know? We've never had a new teacher before."

"That's what I mean. Who is she? Why would she want to live out here in the middle of nowhere at the last minute like this? No one new ever comes here."

"She needed a job. She's probably so stupid no other school would hire her."

Lewis shook his head. "It's suspicious. Everything could change. What if she's not stupid? What if she's *smart*?" This was an excellent question. Lottie and Lewis depended on being significantly more clever than their teachers. "I'm telling you there's going to be something diff —"

Lewis suddenly stopped talking. Lottie looked over her shoulder to see who was coming. Lewis had stealth radar when it came to talking. If anyone but Lottie came within earshot, he instantly clammed up. Sure enough, Betsy Pelican had come around the post office hedge and was gaining on them.

Lewis didn't say another word as the three of them walked to school and Betsy chattered about her family's vacation trip to Missouri. Then Betsy tossed her long blond ponytail and announced that she had met their new teacher at the Main Street Feed Store over the weekend. Her name was something French. "She bought one hundred pounds of Harvest Hill Senior Dog Food," Betsy said knowingly, pleased to be a source of information.

"Is she nice?" Lottie asked. "Is she smart?"

Lewis nodded, wanting to know.

"She's . . . different," Betsy said. "She's hard to describe." And they climbed up the steps of the Oxford United School.

The new teacher was waiting for them in Room 11. She wasn't exactly young or old or tall or short. She was pretty, but you couldn't quite say why. Her hair was pulled back in a soft bun. She wore small tortoiseshell eyeglasses and had lots of wrinkles around her green eyes — like a person who smiles all the time. But she didn't smile at them as they came into the room. She just watched them, greeting them with her eyes. She was very serious. The sixth graders came in noisily but then quickly settled down when they saw her.

Only when all twelve of the students had entered did she smile. Briefly. Then she turned and wrote her name on the chalkboard. *Ms. d'Avignon.* She called the roll and seemed to be sizing up each of them as they answered. When she called Lewis's name, he just raised his eyebrows and looked at her. "Lewis Weaver?" she asked again. Lewis nodded once. The class tittered. Ms. d'Avignon inhaled deeply and looked her students over from head to toe, making notes on a small clipboard.

"Welcome to sixth grade," she finally announced. "My records show that you are all eleven or twelve years old. By now, I expect that you know just about everything there is to know." The class laughed nervously. Ms. d'Avignon didn't.

"To make sure of it," she continued, "I would like each of you to write an essay for me titled 'Everything I Know.'"

Most of the sixth graders groaned.

"Essays?" whimpered Alan Wolf. "My brother told me sixth grade would be multiple choice. . . ."

"I'll give you a month to work on it, because I want to see a lot of effort."

Lottie chewed the end of her new pen and thought about knocking off this essay during lunch hour. It was such a vague assignment that pretty much anything she wrote should be good enough. She'd draw up a little list of her favorite subjects, mention some books she'd read, and wrap it up with a summary of her chores at home. Everything she knew! She yawned. Lewis was wrong to worry. Sixth grade would be no different.

Ms. d'Avignon called on Janice Forester who, as usual, was holding her hand up straight into the air like a flagpole. "If you don't tell us how many pages it should be, some of the kids in here won't write more than a paragraph. How many pages should it be, Ms. d'Avignon?"

"That depends, Janice. How much do you *know*?" Ms. d'Avignon challenged. She looked around the room and — Lottie felt certain — she locked eyes with Lottie Cook. "Start at the beginning. Begin with your earliest memories." Ms. d'Avignon still didn't exactly smile. But Lottie sure did.

Earliest memories? Suddenly something happened. A switch had flipped. Lottie was almost glad she was there. She was excited to do her homework. She beamed at Lewis. Lewis blinked back. His head was tilted and his mouth was relaxed.

He was asleep.

Throughout the day Ms. d'Avignon conferenced with

the students one on one. She started at the end of the alphabet, first Alan Wolf, then Lewis Weaver. When he was called Lewis was still sleeping, so Lottie shot a spit wad at him while she pretended to cough. (They all believed they could get away with anything in class if they caused a small distraction by pretending they were coughing.) Lewis straightened his head and moved forward with remarkable composure. Several classmates chuckled as they anticipated Ms. d'Avignon's attempts to converse with Lewis.

"Is something funny?" Ms. d'Avignon asked the class over her shoulder. They all fidgeted innocently and pretended to cough. The teacher looked back at Lewis, who returned her steady gaze. "Lewis Weaver. I've been warned all about you," she said in a low steady voice. "I've suggested that your speech therapy on Fridays be canceled. I think your time can be put to better use in here. Do you have any problems with that?"

Lewis shook his head calmly, but his wide eyes widened.

"I couldn't care less whether you decide to speak in the sixth grade or not. Your classmates will make more than enough noise to compensate. Frankly, nodding and shaking your head can take you a long way in this life, as I'm sure you've already discovered. Academically I intend to focus on your strengths, which I gather are music, math, and science." Lewis blinked and nodded. Then he actually smiled — something he had never done for a teacher before. Ms. d'Avignon smiled back.

When Ms. d'Avignon called Janice Forester to her desk at the front of the room, the class almost gasped out loud as they watched her conference take place. Janice's perpetually steely posture sagged, gradually but distinctly, until she was literally slumping in her seat. Even her poker-straight braids seemed to wilt. The class couldn't hear what was said, but from what Janice told Betsy later, it had something to do with the sad consequences of being a tattletale and a know-it-all.

"Charlotte Cook," Ms. d'Avignon called. Lottie didn't care that the class was snickering at her full name while she walked to the teacher's desk. "Is something still funny out there?" the teacher asked again, icily.

"They call me Lottie," Lottie shrugged.

"My mother's name is Charlotte," said Ms. d'Avignon quietly. "That's what I'd rather call you."

Lottie blinked. Taken off guard, she nodded.

"Your grades have always been mediocre," Ms. d'Avignon said, flipping through her clipboard, "except when they have been superlative. Explain that to me."

Lottie spoke before thinking. "School is boring usually," she said, loudly enough for the rest of the class to hear and gasp.

Ms. d'Avignon glared over her shoulder at the coughing class before locking eyes with Lottie again. "Not anymore," she said. "I expect your essay to be the most insightful in this class. I do *not* expect that you can finish it during your lunch hour."

Lottie's jaw was on the floor. How could the teacher possibly know she'd been thinking about lunch hour? She didn't know what to say. Ms. d'Avignon continued, "Sixth grade will be as interesting as you make it, Charlotte Cook. I am expecting it to be fascinating." Then, surprisingly, Ms. d'Avignon smiled. Lottie smiled back. And together they *laughed*. The class murmured and coughed wildly. Except for Lewis, of course, who looked . . . relaxed . . . again.

As Lottie walked back to her desk she felt as though her head was filling slowly with helium until she was walking on air. She was glad she went to school. Unbelievable. She was glad to be in the sixth grade, and she thought Ms. d'Avignon was the most intelligent person she had ever met. Sixth grade was clearly something at which she would excel. She felt like she was glowing.

At supper her father nearly choked on his corn on the cob when Lottie announced, "I loved school today."

As Lottie described her day, the meal turned into a feast. Lottie and her father raided the cellar for preserves and syrups. They made corn bread pancakes, fluffed with real whipped cream and drenched in sticky sweet sauces. Mr. Cook sizzled bacon and squeezed oranges. Lottie boiled pink applesauce — her own secret recipe — and sprinkled everything with nasturtiums while she told her father about the new teacher and how the world had changed in an instant. He beamed, he glowed, he hung on every word she said.

Later, as he tucked her in, Mr. Cook asked Lottie to tell him a story like she used to when she was little. He had so missed the crickety sound of her voice helping him remember things.

Lottie squinted her hazel eyes, smiled, and took a deep breath. Thinking of the essay she was going to write, she said, "I'll start with one of my earliest memories." And then . . .

Nothing. Lottie's mind was blank.

Mr. Cook, his eyes on the glow-in-the-dark constellations on Lottie's ceiling, hadn't realized what was wrong. "Go on, then, Lottie, tell a nice quiet one."

A moment slipped by, and then another, and then Lottie sobbed. Lottie, who almost never cried, sobbed so loudly that her father fell clean off her loft bed and nearly broke his ankle when he tried to land on his feet. Lottie's sobbing shook the rickety bed, and she buried her face in the pillows.

"I c-can't!" she cried. "I've forgotten!"

Mr. Cook felt like crying himself, on account of his ankle. He hobbled around under the loft and tried to walk off the pain. "Lottie, don't cry now! You'll remember. You will!"

"All I know is the capital city of Ecuador and the year the Treaty of Paris was signed! All I know is th-the square root of one hundred and forty four!"

Down below the loft bed, where Lottie couldn't see him, Mr. Cook allowed himself a deep, satisfied smile. "Don't worry, don't worry!" he muttered as he hobbled out of the room and all over the house looking, searching. . . .

It was a difficult house to search, and Lottie's sobs echoed off the crooked walls for nearly half an hour. The house had once been just two square rooms, more than a hundred years ago. Since then it had been added to and expanded in a haphazard sort of way. By the time Lottie was grown there were more than a dozen crooked rooms, depending on how you counted them. (Once, for instance, when Lottie was two and the autumn leaves were especially brilliant, she and her father slapped a tiny extra room onto the back of the house to accommodate the thousand or so leaves that she collected and soaked in glycerin.)

That night while Lottie cried and cried, Mr. Cook searched all the strange rooms they had built: the Leaf Room, with its floor of soft leaf mulch; the Mud Room out back, with a dirt floor and waterproof walls; the Spinning Room; and the

Miniature Room and Giant Room, which were very nearly magical.

Finally Mr. Cook found what he was looking for. In the Giant Room, beneath an enormous footstool, he found three rain boots, his missing truck keys, a massive flashlight, and the StoryBox. Its rich cherry color was still gleaming.

He carried it back to Lottie's room without looking inside. He managed to get himself up the wobbly ladder with his now swollen ankle, and pushed the shining box toward the shuddering bundle of Polartec pajamas that was Lottie.

"This should help."

Lottie looked up. The sight of the box made her gasp. A moment went by. Then another. She looked at her father's round hopeful eyes. She had never felt worse. Not only had she forgotten every single story she had ever wanted to treasure, but now she had to break his heart. She opened the box and showed him. When the lid came off, the whole room shimmered slightly.

But the box was empty.

His expression didn't seem to change. He was waiting. Lottie nudged the empty box toward him and sniffled out her words. "I didn't use it. Not a single thing in there. It's too late. You were right all along. I don't remember anything important anymore. And now I'll fail sixth grade because I have nothing to write! I'm not going back."

But Mr. Cook was still smiling at her. Looking a little too pleased with himself in Lottie's opinion. Didn't he understand what she was telling him? "Try it," was all he said. He hobbled back down the ladder, and with one last smile over his shoulder he limped out of the room.

Lottie collapsed on the bed. By now she had no tears left. The room was dark, but there was definitely a warm cherry glow coming from inside the empty box. Lottie tried to ignore it and just fall into a miserable sleep, but she found that she couldn't. Her eyes kept opening and drifting back to the box. Finally she pushed the lid back into place to block the glow, but it still seemed to be seeping from under the edges.

Lottie wasn't sure how much time had passed. Alone in a dark room, aching for sleep to come, it is very hard to keep track of time. But she was quite certain that it was the middle of the night when she heard something . . . a quiet rustling sound that was definitely coming from inside the box.

Lottie sat up in her bed, her heart suddenly racing. With her rational side she tried to calm herself down. *You must have trapped a moth in there,* she told herself. *A big, giant gypsy moth,* she persisted as the rustling sound grew stronger. *Take off the lid; shoo it out,* she thought. *Don't be silly.* She reached out her hand and touched the lid.

It wasn't quite the same as static electricity, but Lottie would later say that it felt almost like touching a doorknob on a cold winter morning and feeling the sparks rush into your hand. She lifted the lid and —

A big double fistful of something, a flurry of color, came swirling straight at her face. Lottie tried screaming, but couldn't. She cringed back, and it missed her by inches, veering off to the left toward her open window. It smashed full force into the screen and rebounded toward her dresser, where it made some sort of a landing. Now, as it noticed its own reflection in the dresser mirror, Lottie was able to get a good look at it.

It reminded her of a bird, about the size of a crow, with deep black eyes on either side of a beak. It stretched its wings and walked around on the dresser, poking at various things. Yes, it definitely was a bird, with scratching, three-toed feet. The problem was its color. Colors. This thing was every possible color. Nothing like a rainbow, more like the way a box of crayons looks after you've dumped all the crayons out, broken quite a few, and peeled off most of the wrappers.

The bird noticed something in the mirror and looked back over its shoulder at Lottie's bulletin board. It squawked in a pleased way and hurtled itself across the room, just barely missing the overhead light. Pecking at the many layers of artwork, dating back to a two-year-old's scribbles at the very bottom, the bird seemed satisfied. Then it turned to Lottie.

"There you are!" it said. It was very clearly speaking. It spoke much better than it flew, and it took Lottie a second to be surprised that it could talk.

"H-hello. Bird," she stammered, and then, trying to be friendly, she sort of whistled . . . the way people do when they want the attention of a trained parrot.

The bird laughed and whistled back. Lottie stared. She whistled again, feebly. The bird barreled over to the lid of the cherry wood box and cocked its eye at her. "*Squawk!* I've waited years and you're just going to whistle at me, Lottie Cook?"

Lottie was speechless.

"Oh, bygones!" it squawked. "No time now!" The bird took Lottie's little finger in its tickly claw and urged her closer to the box. At this point it didn't really occur to Lottie to resist. She felt herself floating along after the bird as if in a dream. In some ways she thought she actually was dreaming. But she was not.

"Watch your big pointy head," it chirped, delighted to see that Lottie was cooperating. And there they went . . . into the box.

Lottie had the lovely slow-motion feeling of falling in a dream. The suspense went on and on, and she wondered why she didn't jerk herself awake like usual. The longer they traveled, the more she sensed that they weren't going down exactly. The bird's little claws gripped Lottie's finger tightly, and she felt its wings twitching in a hundred different directions. Flying clearly wasn't its specialty, but it didn't seem to make a difference now. However the bird flapped and fluttered, the only direction they seemed to take was *through*. Through dark, warm swirls of cherry wood. Then through changing clouds and skies. Then through leaves, blossoms, branches, until they landed at the bottom of a young tree in bloom.

Lottie lay in the clover and looked up. She knew exactly where she was. One deep breath and she could smell the cherry blossoms of her favorite tree. *The one her father had definitely cut down.* But there it was. And as the breeze waved the branches she could hear the sound of her mother's song. She thought she had forgotten! She remembered it all now, because there it was. The tree grown from the seed her mother had spit from the kitchen window before Lottie was born.

It's the best dream I ever had, Lottie thought. Staring up at her tree, she smiled. She knew she would never forget this story again as long as she lived. She didn't want to move because she was afraid of waking up.

"*Squawk,*" interrupted the bird from one of the lower branches, just inches from Lottie's ear. "What time is it? Can't be too careful," the bird squinted at the sun, which was still above the western cornfields beyond the barn. "I'd say five o'clock. If it's summer, hard to say. Definitely afternoon. Or later! *Squawk.* Can you tell time, Lottie Cook?"

Lottie felt like she was moving in slow motion as she sat up and looked the strange creature in the eye. "Why are you in my dream?" she whispered, still not wanting to wake up.

The bird's neck feathers were all puffed up. It blinked at Lottie and then it whistled in a plain, ordinary parrot sort of way. Twice. Lottie hesitated and then slowly stretched out her hand. "Who *are* you?" The bird flopped into Lottie's palm, laughing.

"I'm Umber. Thought you'd know. I'm not a dream."

"You're not?"

"Cherry tree! *Squawk!* Not just the tree, you know. Other things to do."

Lottie squinted at the strange creature. "Your name is *Umber*?"

"Actually no. Much longer: Burnt Umber, Blue, Green, White, Periwinkle, Sienna, Turquoise, Rose, Yellow, Evergreen, Black, White, Silver, Midnight . . ." Umber rattled on. Lottie felt her earliest memories rushing back into her mind as she listened to the bird.

The sun slipped behind the corn silos on the western hills and Umber shuddered. "What time do you think it is? We need a place to hide before dark."

CHAPTER TWO

LightLand

Lottie scampered after Umber as the bird bounced through the cornfields, squawking constantly. ("We'll get there in time. Never fear! On we go, that's a girl!") Lottie studied the countryside as they made their way through it.

Memories kept flooding back until Lottie felt like a bathtub that shimmered with water swelling to the very top. She had *all* her stories back now, she felt sure of it. In her giddy happiness, she called out a few memories to Umber as he moved along ahead of her.

"I remember . . ." she called, noticing a bee buzzing nearby, "I remember when Lewis and I were five and we saw the fattest bumblebee ever — Umber?"

"*Squawk!*"

"Buzzing on a patch of clover and Lewis said, 'Bees do

not sting me. Ever. Watch' — and he put his bare foot down right on top of that bee!

"Well, bees do sting Lewis after all," Lottie panted, "and he is *allergic* to them. His foot swelled to the size of a cantaloupe!"

Lottie laughed, remembering, and launched into another story and another and another. She remembered all of them. Everywhere she looked, stories came to mind. Places she'd been. Things she'd done. She remembered eleven years' worth of stories. And as she hurried on, following Umber, she almost felt as if she were watching the memories happen again. The stories were coming back to life in hazy, shimmery images. And as Lottie ran on, the visions faded but the memories did not. They were sharp in her mind in a way that she knew would never fade.

Everything around her looked more or less like the actual countryside around her actual house. And yet it was completely different somehow. When she called this out to the bird, he responded with a befuddling "Yes! Precisely! Nothing's ever just the same twice, is it?"

Through the rows of corn Lottie thought she saw herself, much younger, twirling in the opposite direction, carrying something. It looked so real, almost *solid*. She wanted to get closer and see. "Slow down, Umber!" she called, but the bird didn't seem to hear. The vision was gone when she looked again, but the memory was back. That was the day she had caught her first fish. Lottie tried to keep up with the bird while she felt again how thrilled she had been with the small speckled trout.

It began to look like dusk. The visions were difficult to see. Lottie fought back a yawn; she was getting tired. After all, in *real* Iowa it was the middle of the night. Just when she was ready to quit the chase completely, the bird whispered, "Psst! Psst! Now!" and dropped like a stone, vanishing altogether.

"Hey!" Lottie called, but there was no squawk in reply. Lottie hesitated, looking around. The sun was much lower now. As she squinted behind her and realized that she had no idea where she was, the ground beneath her shook and fell away. Now Lottie was the one to drop like a stone.

She opened her eyes as she landed with a pleasant thump into a soft puffy something. It was an armchair, deep red velvet with enormous cushions, wonderfully comfortable except for a small lump beneath her —

"Squawk!" Umber wriggled out from under her, and now Lottie sank even deeper into the velvety cushions. She peered around in amazement.

She was in a cozy little stone room. The masonry walls were lined with shelves and shelves of books. There was a quiet, crackling fire in a blue stone fireplace. Strange words were carved in the stone. There were ten or twelve enormous velvety armchairs of different deep colors arranged around the fire. Each chair, like Lottie's, was soft and cushiony enough to sleep in, and in fact, in most of the chairs someone *was* sleeping. In one an old man with a long white beard was snoring softly. In another a litter of kittens slept sprawled all over their fat mother cat. In the emerald green chair, a woman with glowing yellow hair sat reading an old leather-bound book. There were several arched doorways, which seemed to lead to long tunnels lit with orange-ish lanterns.

"It's too late now," the bird announced in a whisper. "Too bad. But you'll be back, oh, yes." He happily nestled down into the arm of Lottie's chair. "Safe for the night. We can wait another day, now that we know you've come. Next time you must be earlier. Sunrise! It's going to work, I'm certain of it." He tucked his head under his wing, and Lottie heard him sigh contentedly.

"Hold on," Lottie whispered at him. "What is this place? Who are they? I don't remember any of them, why are they here?" She gestured toward the sleepers.

The bird clucked. "LightLand! Not just for you! In fact it's the opposite — *you* are for *it*!"

"I am for it?"

"Precisely! I waited long. Then I saw the tree. Of course!

Now go to sleep. . . . Sleep until next time." The bird clucked and tsked under its breath and put its head under its wing.

Lottie forgot to whisper. "I can't just go to sleep! I want to know who they are." Umber tried to shush her, but the woman with the glowing yellow hair was watching them now.

"It's NightFall, didn't you notice?" Umber was exasperated. "We took too long. One more day, we can wait. Don't you know this story, Lottie Cook?"

Lottie shook her head and the bird whispered loudly in her ear, "The NightKing."

Lottie's face remained blankly puzzled. Umber looked nervously around the room, cocking his head at the woman watching them with great interest.

"Darkness belongs to him, he prowls, looking for sleepers. . . ."

"What are you talking about?" Lottie scoffed. "Some kind of monster? Night king? I've never heard of such a thing."

The bird stared, horrified. "But there is. He prowls. . . ."

"That's silly. Like the bogeyman? There's no such thing. Is there?" Lottie stammered a little in spite of herself. "The night is, is just the night. There's nothing different there."

The bird laughed in a sad little way and the yellow-haired woman sighed.

"You've brought her after all this time?" she finally asked the bird, who nodded.

"*Squawk!* And years are long!"

"Perhaps you were right then, Umber. Well done."

"She called me! At last, long last, the sign," the bird rattled on.

"Umber was faithful, my dear, he believed in you. We've all hoped, waited, but Umber most of all."

The bird blushed a deep violet color. "Almost gave up! Didn't!"

"But this story, the long story," the woman said to Lottie, "you don't know it?"

Lottie shook her head.

"Let her talk to Robert," the woman announced definitively. "Let Robert explain about LightLand."

"Ohh, it's not nice to bother poor Robert, should we?"

The woman closed her book completely and gave Umber a sharp look. The bird fretted as he hopped over to the chocolate-brown armchair. There was a pair of feet dangling over the side and a low rumbling snoring coming from the cushions. The bird landed on the shoes and chirped softly, "Robert? Sorry to bother you. Wake up, won't you?" With a sort of shrug he turned back to the yellow-haired woman. "No use, is it?" Then to Lottie he added, "It's all sleep now for him, ever since. The best thing for him."

"Robert, wake up," the yellow-haired woman ordered, and the feet waggled in a spastic way. "Robert! I'm talking to you. Now!" The feet pulled back and disappeared as a messy mop of yellow hair rose from the cushions. A pinkish, sleepy face was beneath the mop of hair, and Robert yawned long and loud, squinting. Lottie stared at him as he rubbed his eyes. His long arms and legs unfolded from the chair. He looked almost as tall as her father, but much, much younger. A boy. Sixteen or seventeen years old, perhaps.

"Ahhhww," he stretched and blinked achingly at them. "Wassat? Ohh, Mother, right?"

"Robert," the yellow-haired woman continued pointedly, "this is Lottie Cook. She doesn't know your story. Tell her the story, Robert."

Robert grinned, scratched his head, tugged his earlobes, stretched some more, and shrugged. "Wassat? A story?"

The bird seemed deeply troubled by Robert's predicament. "No matter!" He hopped to the woman's chair and pecked at her hand. She didn't flinch. She kept her gaze on Robert.

"*Your* story, Robert, you know, who you are, where you come from, and that sort of thing," the woman prodded, but her face looked pained.

Robert grinned sheepishly. "Who I am? Right, sorry." He turned to Lottie. "I'm Robert."

Lottie smiled back at him and wondered what the point of all this was. The woman persisted. "Go on, Robert. What else do you remember?"

"Hum. Well, I'm Robert, and there's my mother." Robert looked very pleased with himself.

The woman smiled in the saddest way possible. "That's right, dear. I know you're sleepy, but is there anything else?"

Robert smiled happily and yawned. "Nothing, mmmm, nothing important." He closed his eyes and sank back into the chocolate chair until once again only his shoes were visible. The rumbling snoring started up almost instantly.

The bird tsked and tutted. "Poor Robert. Woke him up for that! Remember the old Robert? Tell a story? Couldn't keep him quiet, could we?"

"Yes, I still remember, but we are the only ones who do," the woman said softly and turned her sad gaze on Lottie. "It's been years now since Robert thought he knew better and stayed out past NightFall. He thought he could get away with it. . . . He greeted us above at dawn boasting of seeing the stars. He said he'd slept in trees and woke with dew in his hair. Heard owls, nightingales, bragged about moon-flowers, lightning bugs, he said. Flies, that light up in the dark!"

"Fireflies!" The bird shook his head. "Bats!" Umber and the woman laughed in a wistful way.

"He was so furious when we didn't believe him. He swore he'd prove us wrong, bring back fireflies for us all to see. But the next dawn, he didn't greet us. We discovered him asleep in a tree. Like this — his memory gone." The woman looked toward her son.

"What happened?" Lottie asked, staring at Robert's dangling feet.

"The NightKing had found him. This is what the NightKing does." The woman sighed and stared helplessly at her hands in her lap.

"The NightKing doesn't sleep!" Umber was agitated. "Never! At NightFall he prowls. Captures the foolish, like Robert."

"Captures? But —" Lottie shook her head. She didn't understand. Robert couldn't have been captured when he was right here.

"With his veil he captures their memories, their inspirations, every significant thought," the woman continued as Umber nodded. "After capture, they no longer remember anything important, and then, well it's just a matter of time until they won't be remembered themselves, you see? To forget is to be forgotten. And in LightLand, to be forgotten is to disappear. Here below we try to remember the old Robert, but daily, the memory slips away more and more, until —"

"*Squawk.*" The bird shook his feathered head furiously.

"She needs to know, Umber. Until he'll vanish. He'll be lost to Oblivion. Existence worse than death. Oblivion."

Lottie squirmed uncomfortably.

"My Robert has been very lucky. We protect him here in the NightRoom and try to keep him with us. Perhaps some-day soon there will be hope for Robert. For the others like him . . ."

"Lottie Cook!"

"Umber hopes that you may be able to help, my dear."

"Me? But how? Why me?"

"Cherry tree!" Umber nodded. He and the woman ex-changed looks.

Lottie wrinkled her forehead. Nothing they said made sense to her. What could *she* possibly do to help Robert?

She glanced around the small room once again. "You all live here — underground — all the time?"

"No, Lottie Cook, in the daylight we're safe above. When the sun is up, the NightKing is quiet, they say. He enters a trance. Usually. Living this way, we manage to evade him. Before, he took dozens of victims each night."

"Where are those people, the other ones he captured?" Lottie asked, shivering. She curled up in her red armchair and hugged her knees. Somehow she felt safer in the velvety softness.

"Gone. Forgotten. Oblivion," Umber rattled.

"Their voices may still echo in his fortress, a part of his collection. I imagine some may be guarded, the way we guard Robert."

Lottie shook her head. "But why would anyone want to —"

"It is said that the NightKing has no memory of his own," the woman interrupted. "It's the essence of his evil power: emptiness. He is an empty void, a vacuum in space, prowling at night in search of souls he can absorb."

"Where did he come from?" Lottie asked.

The woman shook her head. "That knowledge has been captured. He controls the reach of our memories by stealing years from our history. We no longer know what happened *Before*. Our memories are hemmed in by fear and by distraction," the woman said, watching her son sleep. "While we use our own memories to guard Robert, we don't have full strength. We can't go on this way much longer. LightLand is suffering."

Lottie found herself shaking her head.

"You don't believe, my dear?"

"I, um . . . well, it's all so . . . I don't know. . . ." She frowned. "Was it always called LightLand? Even when you weren't afraid of the dark?"

The woman nodded. "Remembering creates this world, as surely as daylight illuminates it. Oblivion would destroy it as surely as darkness overtakes light." She gestured toward the words carved in the blue stone of the mantel. *"Nunc Lux, Munc Nox.* Now it is Light, suddenly it is Night."

Lottie didn't understand a word of it. She fought back another yawn.

"She's tired, *squawk,* let her sleep. She'll return! Now she knows the way!"

"Yes, Lottie Cook," the woman said in a fond voice. "Nothing more will happen tonight. Sleep, dream, and you'll find yourself at home."

"But come back! There's much to do here, Lottie Cook!" Umber squawked importantly.

Lottie was desperately tired but found herself strangely anxious. Not that she actually believed all this about the NightKing, but still . . . "Is it safe? To sleep?"

"So you do believe?" The woman smiled.

Lottie felt her cheeks turn red and hot.

"Oh yes, of course, my dear," the woman continued, obviously pleased. "It is very safe to sleep here, below. These NightRooms were carved out after the NightKing first came to power. We were all forced below ground, and these caverns and tunnels were built in secret all across the Great Valley. Everyone in LightLand went into hiding. Except *his* creatures."

"The rats! And mice, most of them," Umber rattled.

"In those early times, we hid day *and* night. We didn't know the limits of his terror. . . ."

The woman's voice went softly on with the story of the NightKing. The soft, velvety chair, the warmth of the fire, the gently lit room . . . However hard she tried to resist it, Lottie's eyelids were too heavy to keep open, her arms too heavy to stir. She felt the small stone of a cherry seed in her hand. Lottie began to sink into a warm, deep sleep, still hearing the voices fluttering around her.

"*Squawk.* She didn't know the story. Thought one of them would've told her."

"And now she's barely heard the half of it."

"The cherry tree, that was the sign! When I saw it, I knew."

The smell of blossoms, the swirl of branches, Lottie saw them all again in her mind. The rediscovered memories mingled around her tree as she drifted into a dream.

And Lottie Cook was asleep.

CHAPTER THREE

Lewis's Essay

Mr. Cook couldn't wake Lottie for school in the morning. He had overslept a little himself. His ankle still hurt, and he didn't climb all the way up her ladder. When Lottie barely shifted on her pillow he mumbled, "Five minutes, Lottie, then breakfast." He saw the StoryBox peeking out from under her head. In her sleep, Lottie's hands reached under her pillow to hold on to it. He hovered there for a minute, beaming at his daughter and wondering if he dared ask any questions. *Probably not,* he thought to himself, and he shuffled off to take corn muffins out of the oven.

He gave her a full half an hour before trying again. "Lottie? Lottie, it's getting late." Lottie only murmured in the quietest way, and Mr. Cook had to smile again. He let her sleep, not that he had much choice in the matter.

By this time Lewis was in the kitchen, helping himself to a still-warm corn muffin and wondering where everyone was. Usually he was the one running late.

"Lewis? Is that you?" Mr. Cook called, and Lewis smiled to himself, shaking his head.

Who else would it be? Lewis thought. Of course, he didn't answer.

"Isn't today Friday? I thought you had speech therapy today," Mr. Cook called from another part of the house. "Oh, right! Lottie told me! New teacher, nearly forgot. I'm coming, Lewis, hold on. . . ."

Lewis just sat munching his muffin, leaving conspicuous corn crumbs all about the kitchen. The Cooks' kitchen was always spotless, yet no one had ever been seen mopping, or vacuuming, or washing dishes. These things just always seemed to be done already. (Lottie and Lewis assumed that Mr. Cook must stay up at night to do these chores. They decided not to ask him about it, for fear that it would ruin this very pleasant system. What if he suddenly wanted them to do the dusting?)

Mr. Cook limped slightly as he came into the small yellow kitchen. Lewis noticed and raised his eyebrows. "Twisted my ankle last night. Nothing serious. Lottie is still asleep."

In response to Lewis's tilted head, Mr. Cook shook his, smiling. "No, no, she's not sick, I'm quite sure. Just tired. It was a big night. We feasted! I imagine she told you the news: Lottie likes school! This new teacher . . . why, I wouldn't be surprised now if she decided to wear actual clothes. I'll go wake her up." Mr. Cook trotted gamely off again and Lewis followed, leaving a trail of crumbs behind him all the way to Lottie's room.

She hadn't moved at all. Her father called her name sweetly. He nudged her, smiled at her, and then climbed back down the ladder of the loft bed. "I think I'll let her sleep. Missing a little school, well, after all, she needs her sleep. I'll send a note. Perhaps she'll come in at the half-day."

Lewis glared and climbed the ladder himself. He did not like going to school without Lottie. She would have to be quite ill before he would skip off without her. Being a little sleepy did not impress Lewis as a decent excuse. He shoved her shoulder and tugged her hair; she didn't seem to notice. Then Lewis saw the bright, shiny cherry wood box beneath her pillow. He turned to make sure that Mr. Cook had left the room. He had.

"Lottie!" Lewis hissed right into her ear. "That's enough now." Then Lewis pulled the box out from under Lottie's head.

Lottie sat bolt upright, her eyes popped open, and she gasped. This so startled Lewis that *he* nearly fell off the ladder. "For Pete's sake, Lottie! Nearly gave me a heart attack.

You know, we're late for school as it is. You'll have to wear those same pajamas. You can eat on the way, your father made muffins."

But Lottie hadn't followed Lewis down the ladder. She was still sitting in bed, holding the box. There was a strange look in her eyes. She tilted the box slowly from side to side, listening to a small rolling, rattling sound coming from within.

"Lottie!" Lewis was exasperated, "what *is* that?"

"That," said Lottie quietly, "if I'm not mistaken, is a cherry seed."

"What's going on, Lottie?" Lewis hounded Lottie the whole way to school. She kept yawning. "Why are you so tired when you slept an extra hour?"

They saw no one — they were very late — so he kept talking right until they reached the big double oak doors at the front of the brick building. Lottie had said very little, and had barely nibbled at her muffin. "What's the deal with the box, then?" Lewis hissed as he pulled on the doorknob.

Lottie smiled and blinked at him as he finally clammed up. Lottie didn't mean to keep secrets from Lewis. She simply wasn't prepared to tell everything that had happened the night before. Not yet. She finally whispered to him as they walked the quiet hall to their classroom, "It's Friday, Lewis. Let's see if you can sleep over tonight." Then she patted him cheerfully on the head as if he were a puppy, and they entered the classroom.

Ms. d'Avignon was reading aloud from an old leather-bound book. The class, which normally would snicker and point when kids walked in late, didn't even seem to notice as Lottie and Lewis slunk into their seats. Incredibly, the other sixth graders were completely engrossed in what Ms. d'Avignon was reading.

It was an old journal. It was Ms. d'Avignon's old journal from when she was their age. It was about everything she knew. Lottie thought about the essay she had to write. Everything had changed last night. She knew much more now than she had before.

By the time Lottie had settled herself and looked up, Ms. d'Avignon had closed the journal. Lottie was disappointed and looked over at Lewis to see if he was still awake. He was, and it was a good thing, because Ms. d'Avignon had turned her attention to him. The teacher smiled at him. Lewis smiled back. Then she nodded and said, "Lewis, glad you made it here. Let's have a report on how you are beginning to prepare your essay."

For a second the class half-expected Lewis to speak, then they remembered that this was *Lewis.* Lewis, however, didn't seem fazed. He smiled again and walked calmly to the chalkboard. Lottie held her breath. Lewis took the chalk and began.

Now Lewis knew how to write just fine. When he had to take an exam or write a book report, he had no trouble. He just didn't write to *communicate,* to express himself personally. He only wrote in the academic sense. So an assignment like Ms. d'Avignon's was troublesome for him. It was both an academic requirement and a request for personal expression, communication.

In his own mind, as he stood up from his seat that day, he quickly planned to write on the board an outline, a list of factual information without referring to himself personally. But for some reason, that's not what he did when he arrived at the front of the class.

In the top right-hand corner of the chalkboard he quickly drew what looked like a small explosion. The dashes and dots and squiggles that radiated from it were quite familiar to most of the class. These were the same sorts of symbols that Lewis used to fill his little notebook every day, but on a much larger scale. Lewis took his time, his brow furrowing once or twice. The class was quite riveted. They only took their eyes off Lewis when they simply had to sneak a look at Ms. d'Avignon to see how she was taking this, this *expression* of Lewis's essay.

Ms. d'Avignon wasn't smiling. She wasn't frowning. She was just watching. When Lewis finally stopped, in the lower left-hand corner, and placed the chalk in the tray with a quiet clink, she nodded at him and he sat down. He had a wild, startled look in his eyes as he glanced around. He shrugged nervously at Lottie.

"Well," their teacher said, turning to the class, "what do we make of this?" They sat silently, trying to avoid her gaze. "Alice, suppose you were an archaeologist, hundreds of years in the future, and you stumbled across this. . . . What would you think?"

Alice Atwell was a quiet wisp of a girl. Certainly, she spoke more than Lewis, but not *much* more. She sat twirling her long, straight black hair, studying the board as if this were a math problem to solve. Alice was very good at solving math problems.

Brian Goode whispered loudly to Alan Wolf, "I'd think that I'd dug up an old insane asylum." Alan snorted.

"Thank you for your opinion, Brian," Ms. d'Avignon said without turning her head to look. "We'll hear from you next. Alice?"

"There's a change," Alice said simply.

Alice stood up. She walked to the board and stretched her hand to the upper right-hand corner. "I would know

49

that this was the beginning even if I hadn't seen him do it," she continued.

"There's like a big bang or something first. Here. And then the story moves this way. It's difficult — see the sparks dragging backward? But there's a steady force pulling things along. Gravity or time? Destiny. Pulling everything along with it, leaving this trail along behind. There's a fortress, a tower. With someone in it, see here? And this looks like night, with stars. I think. It *is* a story . . . like this, 'Once, in a land of light, there was darkness and something impossible happened. Though it was unbelievable, it was real. The tower held the secret. And then it was destroyed. After that everything seemed different. It was destined to be so. . . .'" Alice finished, her voice tapering off.

Lottie was staring at Alice. *In a Land of Light.* Had she really said that? Alice met eyes with Lewis, smiled, and then seemed to remember who she was. She blushed, scurried to her seat, and became very busy looking for something in her desk.

The class was dumbstruck. On the one hand, for just a split second, everything Alice had said seemed right, now that you looked at it. On the other hand . . . well for heaven's sake! It was just Lewis's same old squiggles. How could it mean anything? And what had gotten into Alice Atwell?

"Well!" Ms. d'Avignon concluded, looking pleased, her

hands in the air. "Who else? Right, Brian Goode. You were saying?"

Brian Goode appeared a little green around the edges as the class turned to look at him. He cleared his throat a few times and squinted at Ms. d'Avignon. "Um, see, I didn't see that stuff at first, I, uhh."

Brian stood up, as if she'd pulled a string at the top of his head. He slumped up to the front of the room and looked at Lewis's masterpiece. "I'd, um, I'd think, jeez, somebody, like, worked a long time on this, and you know, in the end, it, um, was just sort of, um, nothing. Just a bunch of wacko scribbles."

Again, the class sat stunned as Brian returned to his desk. That was right too, wasn't it? They looked at Ms. d'Avignon, who was beaming. "Well, Lewis, two very different inter-pretations. How is that possible?" Lewis certainly didn't answer. The rest of the class squirmed, hoping that they wouldn't be asked next. Lewis was glancing curiously back at Alice.

"The fact is, it's always possible. No matter how precisely we express ourselves, there is always this room for interpre-tation. The author" — Lewis raised his eyebrows as he was addressed — "must decide how much room he or she wishes to leave. Lewis Weaver, your abstract expression here has left a great deal of room.

"When you compose your essays, keep this in mind:

There are many, many ways to tell the same story. And there are many, many ways to *understand* the same story."

Lewis frowned. Ms. d'Avignon laughed. And they all jumped about a mile when the school buzzer buzzed, summoning the class to the gym for physical education.

Coach Haggler was waiting.

Coach Haggler had always had it out for Lottie. He wasn't keen on comfort and every time she came into the gym, wearing her fuzzy pajamas, his lip curled.

"Pajama Girl!" he bellowed as she walked into the gym. "No sneakers?" Now, Lottie never wore sneakers to school. She wore slippers. Nice, rubber-soled slippers, but *still.* As far as Lottie knew, she and Coach Haggler had reached some sort of détente over the sneaker issue: He gave her Unsatisfactory in gym every year; she shrugged it off.

"Gee, I guess I forgot them," Lottie tried to joke. Someone giggled. Everyone else coughed.

"Step outside!" he ordered Lottie back into the hall. The class was watching with interest through the double windows in the gym doors.

Lottie fought back a yawn.

"I'm keeping you after school today, Pajama Girl," he growled. "You're waxing the gym floor for me."

"Oh. Gee, I don't think I can," Lottie retorted, not flinching when he turned purple. (In hindsight, Lottie admitted it would have been better to hold her tongue. After all, she had *years* of P.E. with Coach Haggler ahead of her.) "Looks like you've used up all the wax on your hairdo," she mumbled.

The coach looked like he was going to explode. He raised his hand in the air and for a second Lottie thought he was going to smack her. Lewis sprang out into the hall to defend her. The coach wheeled on him, "Back in the gym, Weaver!"

"What's happening here?"

Ms. d'Avignon had come around the corner.

"She — she . . . nothing," the coach straightened up and tried to sound calm. "I'm disciplining these students."

Ms. d'Avignon raised her eyebrows. "Really? Hmm. Well, it happens that these are just the students I need. You don't mind if I borrow Charlotte and Lewis for a bit, do you Coach Haggler?" The teacher didn't really wait for an answer. She turned Lottie around by the shoulders and walked her down the hall. Lewis trotted along.

The coach stood there stupidly for a minute, trying to think of something to say. "I guess it's all right." He huffed and went back into the gym. The entire class had their faces pressed to the windows. He knocked most of them over on his way inside.

*   *   *

"Were you really coming to get us?" Lottie asked as their teacher walked briskly ahead of them down the hall.

"Certainly I was. I need you two to fill out some forms we completed this morning before your late arrival." They reached Room 11 and went back inside. The form was very brief. They could easily have done it at lunch or recess. Lottie and Lewis looked at each other and wondered the same thing: *Why had Ms. d'Avignon rescued them?*

"Now, Charlotte, suppose you tell me what you've done to make Coach Haggler so disagreeable?"

"It isn't my fault he hates me."

Lottie told their teacher about the mistreatment she had suffered in the gym ever since she was a first grader. She told how the coach had used her as a target to teach dodgeball. How he called her Pajama Girl. How he made her run extra laps because she was slow in her slippers. How he gave her detention if he ever caught her in the halls, even if she had a pass to go to the bathroom. . . .

Ms. d'Avignon really listened. Not like an ordinary adult who nods and waits for her own turn to talk. She was *interested.* Talking this way made Lottie feel better.

"In my whole life no one has ever been so mean to me as Coach Haggler," Lottie finished.

"Charlotte, it would be irresponsible if I didn't point out that your remark to him was completely inappropriate. Honestly! *Floor wax?*"

It wasn't until much later that Lottie realized . . . she hadn't told Ms. d'Avignon anything about the floor wax. How had she known?

After school they walked to Lewis's small brown house. Lottie still wasn't saying much. "After dark," she whispered with a mysterious smile, "I'll tell you everything."

They went in through the kitchen door. Mrs. Weaver was whipping egg whites. The old-fashioned Mixmaster was so loud that she didn't hear them come in.

"Mrs. Weaver! *Mrs. Weaver!*" Lottie yelled.

Startled, Mrs. Weaver raised the spinning beaters, and the frothy meringue splattered all over Lewis. His mother was not amused.

"What do you think you're doing?!" she fussed. "And shut that door! Heat isn't cheap you know!" They shut the door and didn't bother arguing that it was warmer *outside* on the sunny September day.

While Lewis silently washed off the egg whites, Lottie asked if he could sleep over at her house. Mrs. Weaver scowled and went back to her recipe without answering.

Lewis dried his face on a dish towel. "You go find Biscuit first and bring her in before you go anywhere," she muttered and turned the Mixmaster back on.

Biscuit was Mrs. Weaver's cat, and she hated Lewis. It was mutual. This cat had scratched and bitten him more times than he could count. She was supposed to be a house cat, but was forever slipping outside and getting lost. She was a singed, smokey color and could hide in shadows right under your nose. Lewis and Lottie scrambled through Lewis's back-yard hissing and clacking sticks together, but there was no sign of the cat.

The Weavers' back field was a mess of rocks and rubble. They had never been farmers, and the place was overgrown and wild. Lewis sat on the corner of a dilapidated stone wall and took off his shoe. There was a pebble in it. Suddenly a smokey gray paw shot out of the shadows and scratched his leg. "Ow! Gotcha!" Lewis had caught Biscuit by the scruff of her neck.

Lottie took the cat inside while Lewis retied his shoe. The pebble that had been in it was unusual. It had a groove in it like a chiseled line. Lewis slipped the strange stone into his pocket and caught up with Lottie, who was calling him from the back porch. She was splattered with egg whites, but Lewis had permission to sleep over.

*   *   *

Lottie and Lewis spent hours after supper that night trying to get Lottie's father to go to bed. But he was dying to ask Lottie about the box. He felt sure that something had happened, because she had such a glint in her eye. Finally as they sat around the wood stove eating hot, salty, buttered popcorn, Lottie smiled almost shyly and asked if anyone wanted to hear the story of the cherry tree. Mr. Cook could not have been any happier, listening to the story that he knew she would remember, and, as if in a magic trance, he fell instantly into the deepest of deep sleeps right there in the rocking chair.

Lewis was fidgeting with the unusual pebble in his pocket. "All right Lottie," he said. "It's dark. Now what's going on?"

Lottie walked slowly to her room and returned with the StoryBox. She held it out to Lewis and then told him the whole story, breathlessly. The box, Umber, the tree, the NightRoom, poor Robert, the NightKing, Oblivion. Then, with real excitement, she opened the lid and took out one smooth and shiny cherry seed.

"What do you think?"

He always absolutely believed Lottie. He leaned over the box and looked in. *Something* had happened to her, that was certain. But . . .

"It could have been a dream," he said.

"It was not a dream," Lottie said firmly.

"It's kind of like school today, isn't it? When I had to write on the blackboard. Different ways to understand the same thing . . ."

"Or not understand," Lottie added impatiently. "I remembered everything again! It had to be magic."

"Are you sure that you didn't dream a wild dream after all the crazy food you ate last night?" Lewis pressed as Lottie frowned. "Or it could be . . . that your father made a, a sort of, kind of hypnotic box that creates, you know, visions. Three-dimensional holograms? Makes you see things. It's probably some sort of mind trick."

"But the cherry seed, Lewis. It's real." She held it out to Lewis. He hesitated, then placed his strange pebble in the StoryBox and took the seed. They were the same size. He rolled the seed in his hands and held it up to the light. He shrugged and Lottie took the seed back. Lewis took his pebble.

"Let's try to get in," Lottie's eyes sparkled.

"Now?" Lewis asked. Of course *now.* Lottie always meant now.

"Maybe he built secret compartments in here somehow," Lewis suggested. They leaned together, looking deep into the glowing cherry wood for some kind of secret. Memories flooded their minds as they peered in. They wondered what might be unlocked if they found their way inside somehow.

And they fell.

Through.

CHAPTER FOUR

In The Dark

It was pitch black. They could feel the rush of wind and see blurred stars as they whooshed through into LightLand. It was late at night. There was no moon at all and the cold air filled their lungs as they landed and gasped. There were stones underneath their feet. Lewis could see Lottie's eyes shining as she stared hard at the darkness, trying to recognize the site.

Now Lottie had not actually been frightened by the story of the NightKing and the babbling Robert. She was almost always brave, and this sort of bogeyman stuff didn't scare her. But Lewis, even hearing it all secondhand, felt queasy. As a little kid, Lewis *had* been afraid of the bogeyman. And he only liked to venture outside on the brightest of nights when moonlight flooded the scene. Finding himself in the middle of a very dark night in the middle of a scary place where it was *dangerous* to be above ground at night was almost too much for Lewis. He gripped Lottie's arm tightly and strained his ears, listening for the slightest sound.

Lottie shook her arm out of reach. Twice. "Get a hold of yourself, Lewis. You're all right. I wonder where we are. . . ."

Suddenly the wind picked up and they heard something.

There was a great creaking, groaning sound coming from directly above them. Lewis could barely breathe. The groaning was *so* loud! And now there was a humming, vibrating sound that shook right through the rocks under their feet.

"Run for it! Follow me!" Lottie yelled, dragging the petrified Lewis behind her out into the darkness.

They couldn't see where they were going, and they tripped and bashed along, crashing right into some kind of bramble bush and scratching up their faces. They thrashed farther away, holding their arms straight out in front of them. Finally they stopped themselves just in time as they were about to smash into some kind of wall. They sank down against it, sucking in the cold air.

They could still hear the strange humming, vibrating sound. "Wh-what the heck is th-th-that?" Lewis panted.

Lottie wished desperately that Umber would appear. But, of course, the bird would be safe and cozy in a NightRoom, somewhere below ground.

A firefly bumbled by and Lottie smiled in spite of herself, thinking of Robert, who had loved the night sky. She calmed down. She took a few slow breaths. This was just the night, she thought to herself, and there was nothing here that wasn't always here. Smiling, she told Lewis so.

Lewis disagreed. "We have *no idea,* Lottie! That could be anything! That could be the NightKing! A monster! ANYTHING." Lewis angrily pulled off his shoe. There was a pebble in it again. He shook it out into his hand and retied the laces. He rolled the small stone in his hand; it felt familiar.

They sat in the dark, listening to the awful sound, which, though far away now, was still very creepy. Lewis was lost in thought but Lottie didn't seem to notice.

"It doesn't seem to be coming any closer," Lottie mumbled. "It sounds like a machine, doesn't it?"

Lewis suddenly dropped the pebble and stood up, listening. Then he turned about, reaching with his hands, feeling, trying to get a sense of where they were. "Lottie," he said slowly, "I know where we are. This is the old stone wall, behind my house. . . ."

Lottie frowned in the dark. "I suppose it *could* be, Lewis, but honestly, there are millions of stone walls in the world. This could be anywhere." Lottie was not impressed.

"That," Lewis said, turning his head toward the mechanical sound, "is the old windmill."

Lottie listened. A windmill? She didn't say anything.

"I remember it, Lottie," Lewis insisted. "From when it used to work."

"It used to work?" All Lottie could remember was a broken, rusting pile of rubble in the back field behind the Weavers' barn. And then, as the wind faded slightly and she heard a deep metallic sigh as the vibrating slowed, she thought she remembered it, too. Ages ago. Before Mr. Weaver had vanished. But it *wasn't* her memory; it belonged only to Lewis.

Before she could say anything there was another sound . . . a motor, a loud roaring. There was a bright light.

They huddled by the wall again, their hearts thumping wildly as something stormed past them and on out through the fields. In the glare of the sudden light they could see each other's faces — scratched, dirty, and frightened — and they could see the long metal arms of the windmill as it spun idly in the slack breeze. Something flew above their heads in the dark. They ducked low to the ground.

"Who. Whoooooooo."

They nearly jumped out of their skins as an owl flew by. The headlights sped past and illuminated a bare, grassy plain.

"What was that thing?" Lottie whispered, standing and brushing the dirt and gravel from her knees. Lewis couldn't move. Lottie pulled him to his feet. "Well, come on, Lewis. It's gone. Let's try and see your windmill."

Lewis caught her arm. "Lottie, I was remembering . . . before we fell through. I was remembering and something came into my mind. This is *my* earliest memory. And it was definitely *not nice.*"

Lottie hesitated. "Look, we have to find out. That's the whole point. Come on. Follow me."

"Last time," Lottie explained as they felt their way forward again, "I got out of this place by falling asleep. So that should be our plan, right? If we get into trouble, we try to go to sleep."

Lewis thought that they were in enough trouble as it was. "What if we *can't*?" he insisted. "I mean, how do we just fall asleep if we're scared to death?"

"Oh, please, Lewis. You can sleep at the drop of a hat."

"What about you?"

"I'll worry about myself! Now come on!"

"Wait!" Lewis was trying to think this through. "Lottie, remember what they told you . . . sleepers are in peril! You were safe sleeping in the NightRoom below ground. We're not *safe* sleeping here, are we?"

This made Lottie pause. "Well, okay, we *won't* fall asleep.

We can do it, Lewis, we'll keep each other awake. We'll stay awake until the sun rises. And then it will be safe to sleep, or we'll find Umber, or something. I mean, really, what choice do we have?"

This was true. So they walked back the way they had just come. Walking through the dark, the terrific noise of the windmill pushed every other thought from their minds. Suddenly, as the wind dropped away and the giant mill groaned to a halt, the moon slipped from behind a cloud bank and they could see.

There were high stone walls surrounding them. The walls formed a wide entrance that they had unknowingly passed through. It was a courtyard, with the windmill as a castle at the other end.

It was a stone tower windmill. It looked almost like a monster, with eight arms wavering in the moonlight. Most windmills have four arms, but this one looked like a giant spider. They shuddered.

Beneath their feet, the hard, lumpy ground was hop-scotched with wide, flat paving stones. The moonlight wavered, but Lottie felt sure that the stones had markings on them. She struggled to understand what was etched on the stone closest to her.

"Lewis! Look, on the stones! It's *your* marks."

The marks on the paving stones did bear a remarkable re-semblance to the squiggles Lewis used in his little notebook, the ones he'd used to draw his essay on the chalkboard that very morning.

Lottie was smiling. Lewis would figure this out! But Lewis was not smiling. Lottie nudged him closer to the stone, and they stared at it together.

"Well?" Lottie finally asked.

Lewis swallowed hard. "It's um, it's a matter of interpre-tation. . . ."

Lottie gritted her teeth. Somehow she had always as-sumed that at least *Lewis* knew what he meant by his cryptic drawings.

"I'm sorry, Lottie, but really. I mean, it's not like it's just a foreign language that you can translate or something."

"Yeah, well Alice Atwell seemed to be able to translate it this morning!"

Lewis shook his head. "It's just a — a — a nervous habit. I don't try to write these things. I just, just *do* it. A lot of days when I get home and the notebook's filled up, I don't even remember doing it at all."

"But what Alice said made sense —"

"I know." Lewis frowned. "It made sense to me, too. But it was *news* to me."

"Well, look." Lottie pointed. "It's all just the same as what you did this morning. See, there's the same squiggle that Alice said was the night, the stars. That's what she said was a fortress. And well, here's the night, the stars, and the fortress itself, don't you think? The windmill is the fortress."

"Maybe it is. . . . I hadn't thought about this in years. At least, I didn't *know* that I had thought about it. This is *my* earliest memory, Lottie," Lewis said quietly. "This was my father's wind lab."

"What's a wind lab?"

Lewis shook his head. "That's what I called it. The windmill and this, this stone yard. It was his. I had forgotten. I've wanted to forget it. You know, he — he — he wasn't . . . well, he wasn't like your dad."

"Oh, Lewis, no one is like my dad," Lottie shrugged.

"He wasn't nice. I'm remembering him now. He was definitely not nice. He used to stay out here in the wind lab. For days sometimes. No one else was allowed in. One time a week went by . . . I was three, I think. I went looking and he had vanished. It was empty. Except for the animals. Laboratory animals. He used them for his experiments. I don't think he took care of them. They were skinny and — and — and — scared-looking. We let them go. But we never saw him again. He was gone. The windmill collapsed a few days later. My mother never said another word about him."

A stiff breeze picked up, and the windmill groaned into action again. Lottie and Lewis shivered simultaneously. "You don't think he's in there, do you?" Lottie asked loudly over the whine of the windmill.

Lewis hesitated. He didn't know why he knew, but he felt certain that his father wasn't there. He shook his head and stuffed his hands into his pockets. He could be wrong, he thought. He nodded and then shrugged, looking down.

"Should we go in?" Lottie asked.

"No," Lewis answered slowly, "but we will. Come on."

They entered the dark windmill through a rusty metal door that Lewis walked straight toward, even in the shadowy dark. They were instantly struck by an eerie, stale odor. A current of air moved thickly through the passageway. It was sour, acidic. It smelled like rotting leaves.

The corridors inside didn't seem to have lights, but they were painted in a weird luminous pale green paint, the color of melted lime sherbet.

Lottie noticed the mice first.

She nudged Lewis and pointed to the darkish crevices where the walls met the floors. There were white mice appearing and disappearing in the shadows up and down the corridor. For all their scurrying activity, they stayed on the edges. Lottie and Lewis kept going.

Around a tight bend in the corridor, an enormous white

rodent skittered across the floor right in front of their feet. "That's the freakiest mouse I ever saw," Lottie gasped.

"That's because it's a rat," Lewis corrected her, pointing out the animal's long, snakey, hairless tail as it vanished.

"Is this all from *your* memory?" Lottie shuddered as a few more rats flickered in and out of sight.

"Shhhh." Lewis didn't answer her. He had stopped walking and had cocked his head, listening. Lottie listened too, and for a minute heard only the unpleasant scratchy sound of mice and rats milling about. But then she heard something else.

For Lewis it was a jumbled whispering, an erratic chorus of voices, and he caught only out-of-context words here and there.

For Lottie it was nearly the same, except . . . except she could hear something she somehow recognized. The sound of a young man's voice, boastful, excited, then proud, insistent. She had heard this voice before. . . .

"*. . . lights! Even in the darkest hour! Stars, I'm telling you, Mother, and the moon, like a bowl of custard, and creatures that light up and fly in the dark like glimmering bumblebees! Fireflies! And other things, beautiful things. Bats that swoop through the air without a sound, owls. You have to see it, all of you, or you've lived half a life —*"

The voice rose and fell and jumbled with other voices and Lottie felt herself almost drowning in the tangle of whispers as she tried to hear more, more of the whispering voice that had surely been Robert's. Before.

What could the NightKing possibly want with these voices? she wondered. The longer she listened the less she heard them.

Lottie didn't know how long she stood there, transfixed, straining for more of Robert's memories. She suddenly jerked when something hopped across the hall and just barely missed crashing into her before it turned and hopped back where it had come from. This time it was a scrawny, flat-eared white rabbit with red eyes.

"Where are all these animals coming from?" Lottie wondered out loud.

"The lab," said Lewis, and he pointed upward.

Lewis was far ahead of her down the corridor, heading into a doorway. It came out into a stairwell. The stairs appeared endless, turning and turning and vanishing in the darkness above their heads. Lottie was getting tired, but she followed Lewis up the stairs. Every hundred steps or so, a rodent skittered under her feet, making her jump and shocking her numb brain awake.

After climbing for what seemed like forever, they reached

a small landing where there was a window, and a bit of smokey moonlight poured through, along with the thinnest wisps of fresh, clean-smelling air. Lottie caught up to Lewis here. He was gazing out the window, breathing deeply. A lazy white rat had settled for a moment at Lewis's feet and it was gnawing on his shoelaces. The staircase still towered over their heads and Lottie wondered if they were only halfway to the top.

The strange whispering seemed louder again now. "It's the NightKing's collection, it has to be," Lottie said. "Other people's stories, memories he's stolen. But why is it in here?"

Lewis moved his lips a little and looked as though he were whispering, too. "I don't know about that," he said, shaking his head. "The stairs, I do remember. I couldn't climb them, I was too small. But Zerox ran ahead, remember? Our dogs. Two of them —"

Lewis was meaning to go on, describe the dogs that Lottie had forgotten all about, but suddenly there was no need. For there they were. Zerox! Two dogs, identical in every way. They bounded up from below on the stairs and leaped onto Lewis, bowling him over, licking him from head to toe. The lazy rat ran for cover, and the whispering was momentarily blotted out by the sound of two astonished children laughing and two dogs barking.

"How in the world . . . where did they come from?" Lottie asked.

"I remembered them!" Lewis exclaimed. "I remembered them and they came. I haven't seen them since . . . that day. Th-they ran out of sight, up the stairs, and we never found them after."

"You remembered them and they came?" Lottie repeated, stroking a shaggy Zerox head. She had a strange look on her face. "You remembered . . . and they came."

Could it work that way? Anything — anyone — that she tried to remember might appear? Could that really be true? And these dogs were not shadowy visions, like the memories she had seen fleetingly when she first came to LightLand alone. They were absolutely solid. Completely real. Lottie wasn't sure about the feeling in the pit of her stomach. And a tingling feeling in her brain. What was it? Her hands actually shook as she numbly stroked the silky back of the dog nearest to her. *Anyone she could remember — could she actually choose?*

The look of pure pleasure on Lewis's face brought her back into the moment. The dogs licked him and whimpered their greeting. Lottie pushed the strange tingling feeling to the back of her mind.

Lewis and Lottie camped there on the landing for a bit,

catching their breath. It was more comfortable than you might have imagined, since each of them had a large, furry dog to lean back against.

They were lost in their own thoughts. The sound of the whispered, stolen memories was blurring more and more in their minds. They were afraid to wonder what would happen if they remembered other things. Afraid to let their thoughts wander away from them. Lottie felt her eyelids drooping.

"Can't sleep . . ." she muttered. "Lewis we have to . . . stay awake. . . ." Lottie tried to shake herself alert, but then found that she couldn't quite remember *why* she wasn't supposed to sleep. Lewis knew, she thought. "Lewis?" Lottie murmured and pried her eyes open to look at him. She looked over at Lewis and saw that his face had tilted and relaxed, eyes open.

"He's already asleep," Lottie mumbled. Too tired to think straight, she let herself nuzzle into Zerox's fur. "We'll be back home then. . . ."

As Lottie sank deeply into a dream, she had two last thoughts: First . . . if Lewis was already asleep, then why could she still see him in LightLand? Second . . . oh, what was it now?

Oh — oh, yes, to be safe they had to stay awake until daybreak.

CHAPTER FIVE

Left Behind

Eldon Cook woke at dawn on Saturday morning, as usual. He had a stiff neck from spending the night in the rocking chair, but he was happy. Lottie was remembering her stories! The box worked. He beamed at his daughter, who was sound asleep on the living room sofa, hugging the StoryBox under her head like a pillow. He forgot to wonder where Lewis was.

The morning slipped by peacefully without Lottie budging from her spot on the sofa. Mr. Cook puttered around, setting the house right while no one was watching him.

Lottie and Lewis had been right not to ask too many questions about the housekeeping. The exceptional tidiness of the Cook household was the benefit of a very modest bit of magic.

Now the truth is that most people are capable of at least

a modest amount of magic. And some are capable of a whole lot more. Eldon Cook needed help housekeeping. One day, when Lottie was a very small baby, he stood there by himself in the middle of the house — and it was the messiest house you could imagine, with piles of dishes, laundry, and dirty diapers in every room — and he *willed*. He willed that the house be clean. He remembered what it was like when the house was really completely perfectly clean. And he willed it back that way. The human will is something magical. He believed that it would be. And it was.

So, as usual that Saturday morning, he hurried from room to room, willing the house clean. He found that it only worked on the parts of the house he actually looked at and concentrated on . . . under furniture and deep closets were areas that remained unaffected. Mr. Cook supposed that if he crawled diligently about and poked into these parts they would be clean as well, but it seemed unnecessary to go to such great lengths.

When he was done Mr. Cook felt the same rush of satisfaction that everyone feels when they've done a good job at something. He finished by fluffing the pillows on the sofa and trying to slip one under Lottie's head. But the instant that he touched the gleaming cherry StoryBox, Lottie sat bolt upright, fully awake.

Like last time, Lottie stared wide-eyed at the box in her hands. It made a different, sliding sound as she rolled it gently back and forth. Lottie peeked inside and gasped.

"Lewis . . ." she croaked quietly.

Mr. Cook was determined *not* to ask about the box, so he turned and headed for the kitchen. "Yes," he called back over his shoulder, "where is Lewis? Did he head home early?"

Lottie didn't answer. She didn't know for certain. But when she opened the smooth cherry lid of the gently glowing box, alongside the cherry seed and a strange-looking pebble, was Lewis's notebook.

Lewis's mother called at lunch to see if he was coming home anytime soon. Luckily Lottie answered the phone and quietly told Mrs. Weaver that Lewis wanted to sleep over again if it was okay. Fortunately it *was* okay, since Lewis was absolutely nowhere.

Lottie walked around in a stupor all morning. What had gone wrong? Lewis had fallen right asleep . . . she was sure of it! It had worked perfectly for Lottie, why not for Lewis? Had the NightKing found him? It couldn't be true. . . .

The minute her father went to town to buy cream for supper Lottie opened the magic StoryBox on her bedroom floor. It looked impossibly small in the daylight. How could she get back inside? She held her breath and tried to fall into it. Clunking her head on the hardwood sides, she started to panic. She tried again. And again.

And again.

She locked her bedroom door for the first time in her life and tried all afternoon to unlock the magic of the box. She had lumps on her head and her heart was racing when her father knocked, asking her to set the table.

At supper Mr. Cook wondered what had gotten into his daughter when she poured vinaigrette all over a bowl of corn chips and served it like tossed salad. But he didn't say anything; he just ate it. (Actually, it was pretty good.)

"Is there something troubling you, Lottie?" he asked timidly. She shook her head. Mr. Cook drummed his fingers nervously on the tabletop, wondering what to say to her.

Then a little miracle occurred.

The telephone rang, and Lottie, fearing it was Mrs. Weaver again, sprang to her feet and grabbed the receiver. It *was* Mrs. Weaver. "Lottie, I need to talk to Lewis, you put him on the phone this minute," she barked without saying hello.

"Um, oh, okay," Lottie mumbled, her mind racing. Her father watched curiously while she set the phone down, walked in a shuffling circle around the kitchen floor, and picked the phone up again. She breathed deeply into the receiver. "Lewis? Is that you?" Mrs. Weaver barked. Lottie breathed loudly again. "Now listen to me, Lewis, your Aunt Betty Jean has had another gallstone attack. A bad one. And she needs me to come to Peoria right away. Are you listening to me, Lewis?" Lottie breathed heavily and Mrs. Weaver rattled on.

"I may be gone more than a week and I don't want to bring you with me. You'll just get in the way. You ask Lottie's father if you can stay there. I'm leaving in twenty minutes. I'll put the phone number here on the counter, but DON'T CALL ME. It's long distance, understand?" Lottie breathed loudly again, trying with all her might to breathe like Lewis. Mrs. Weaver hung up.

Lottie settled the phone back on the hook with a loud clunk, her head spinning. She had a week. She had a week to get Lewis back.

Lottie stayed up all Saturday night trying to return to Light-Land. Perhaps the problem was the panic that had risen inside her until her eyes were swimming in it. She was nearly hysterical when the sun finally came up on Sunday morning. She fell asleep about the time that her father was doing his morning chores. As curious as he was, he let her sleep.

She was so desperately afraid that the box *wouldn't* work that she may just have been *keeping* it from working. She slept until noon and then tried again. Her father was concerned about all the loud, clunking noises coming from her room.

He finally made Lottie come outside and pick apples with him. While Mr. Cook picked three enormous baskets of shiny red and gold apples, Lottie gnawed on hard, tiny, green ones. *What would happen when Lewis didn't show up for school in the morning?* She had to rescue him before people started wondering. She climbed the oldest tree, a twisted gray tree heavy with beautiful empire apples. These were Lewis's favorites. He had an empire tree in his yard, too. Suddenly Lottie had an idea.

She scrambled out of the tree when her father went to deliver apples to the Arnolds down the road. She ran in the other direction, cut across the field, and was at the Weavers' back door in record time. She found the spare key where Mrs. Weaver kept it on a hook in their empire apple tree.

When Lottie unlocked the kitchen door, Biscuit leaped out of nowhere, yeowling. Lottie had forgotten all about the cat. She put food in the bowl on the floor, and Biscuit eyed her suspiciously as she filled the water bowl.

It was weird to be alone in somebody else's empty house.

Her heart was racing. But no one would know; no one would catch her.

There on the counter was just what Lottie had been hoping for. A note. And it was nearly perfect. It was on gray stationery that read, "Lucille Weaver. Rural Route 9-D. Oxford, Iowa 52322," and then in Mrs. Weaver's tiny, cramped handwriting it read:

Lewis
Gone to Peoria for a week.
Back Saturday.
319–555–5084
DON'T CALL

Lottie took a deep breath. The pen Mrs. Weaver had used was right there on the counter. Lottie used it to insert a tiny, cramped "has" after Lewis's name. The note wasn't signed, but she thought the school would accept it, anyway.

Lottie jumped as Biscuit rubbed against her leg. *Biscuit was actually being friendly?* Lottie shook her head. Everything was upside down. She filled the cat's bowl again and slipped out the door, hanging the key back among the apples.

What if she never found Lewis? What if she never saw him again? Never mind trying to explain to the rest of the world what had happened, what would she do without him?

He had fallen asleep right there in the fortress of the NightKing. Even if she did find him again, what if he was like Robert, without a single memory left? Lottie could hardly see how it would be otherwise.

She was despondent; dread rose in the back of her throat, and it hurt to swallow. She and Lewis had been true friends since they were babies. She simply had to find him. She had to. Back in her room she opened the box on the floor and tried once again to throw herself inside. *Ouch!* She was banging herself up, and it wasn't helping.

She needed to try a new approach. When she lost something her father would always say "Retrace your steps, Lottie." That's what she would do.

"First there was the StoryBox," she said to herself slowly. "Its magic comes out of remembering. Second, there was Umber."

Lottie looked around the room, remembering the crayon bird's bizarre flight through the space. She tried to remember everything about the bird, visualizing each colored feather. She remembered the bird cocking his rainbow head and watching himself in the mirror, then flying over to Lottie's bulletin board, pecking at the papers there. Pecking at the papers . . .

Lottie moved to the crowded bulletin board and leafed back through the faded pages. As she looked, she felt more memories flooding through her mind. The projects, sketches, poems she had created were layered years-thick. Then, there it was.

At the very back, perhaps the very first page ever pinned to the board, a flurry of color caught her eye. It was mostly a multicolored scribble. A sixty-four-color masterpiece. If she hadn't known, she might not have understood . . . but she did. She remembered. She knew just what it was.

It was her first drawing. And it was a bird.

Lottie stood transfixed, prying the page free from under all the other treasures. She felt her face flush. Behind her on the floor, the cherry wood box was wide open and glowing again. Without quite being surprised, Lottie felt a little flutter against her cheek.

"*Squawk.*" Umber made some kind of landing on Lottie's shoulder. "What took you so long?"

"I-I've been trying. . . . I couldn't get in. . . . I've tried *hard.* . . ." Lottie was so relieved to see the bird. As exhausted as she was, she felt hope thumping in her chest. She had done it!

"Oh, bygones!" the bird chirped airily. "You don't *try*, Lottie Cook. You just *do* the thing properly."

"I tried all last night!"

"Exactly wrong. Try *not* trying. In we go, you're needed. The NightKing saw the cherry tree! *Squawk!* Come along."

Umber dove into the box with his claw around her thumb. But Lottie, her mind pounding with thoughts of Lewis, the NightKing, the danger, just clunked her head again. She crumpled onto the floor in frustration. Umber had to come back after her.

"For heaven's sakes, what *are* you doing?" Umber croaked irritably. Lottie sat rubbing her head, which ached terribly.

"Umber, where is Lewis? Have you seen him?"

"Shouldn't say on this side of things." The bird looked nervous.

"What do you mean?! Is he, has he been —"

"Shouldn't get into it from here, we should go! *Squawk!*"

But Lottie simply couldn't. She held Umber's foot and tried to go along. But all she could think was, *What if it doesn't work?*

Lottie put the picture in the StoryBox next to the cherry seed, the stone, and Lewis's little notebook. Turning its pages, she tried in vain to make sense of the squiggles and dots. She thought about his essay. . . . The day Lewis had drawn all of this mess on the board . . . and Alice Atwell had made sense of it. Lottie's eyes blurred as she stared at the chaotic hieroglyphics. She closed the notebook and put it in her pajama pocket. *Maybe I'll understand it in the morning,* she thought. *I'll ask Alice if I have to.*

Lottie reached for the tiny cherry pit. Not really knowing why, she pressed it into the corner of her pajamas and tied a small knot in the fabric to keep the cherry seed there. She did the same with the small stone.

Umber used every trick to encourage her but finally gave up. He wanted to get back to LightLand and he'd have to leave without her. Lottie couldn't follow through the box. It wasn't working. "Oh, well. There's tomorrow, Lottie Cook," the worried bird sighed. "We'll do it tomorrow. But you'll have to stop trying! Never fear, all's well! Not really, but never mind. . . . So, tomorrow, then."

The bird's crazy muttering seemed endless as Lottie squeezed her eyes tightly to block everything out. Umber's squawking vanished suddenly. She opened her eyes, and the bird was gone. Lottie curled into a ball. She didn't know what else to do.

Meanwhile, Lewis had woken up.

He was on the hard stone stairs in the windmill. Lottie, he noticed with a sinking feeling in his stomach, was nowhere to be seen. Zerox, the dogs, sat on either side of him, and he felt somewhat safer knowing they were still there.

Then Lewis looked up. His blood turned to ice water. An

enormous white laboratory rat with red eyes was standing next to him, and it was talking. This thing was three feet tall! It was surrounded by white lab mice that, next to the monster rat, seemed relatively small, though they were at least a foot high each.

"It's him, don't be stupid," one of the mice was whispering fiercely.

"It's not him, where's his wrinkles? Where's his scars?" The rat was scowling and twisting his long whiskers.

"It's a trick! He's testing us! What's he doing with those disgusting dogs?!"

"Be quiet would you?! Want to get us all caged? Or veiled?! You know he hears everything even when he's in his trance."

"Ahhhh!" One of the mice, noticing Lewis's upturned face, was pointing at him and then fell flat on its belly. The others quickly fell too, even the rat, which started whimpering.

"Your Kingship," the rat whined, "your Kingship, we just wondered why you were here on the stairs. Would it please you to come to the tower room? We were just preparing your morning meal. . . . It's not quite ready. . . ."

Lewis didn't know what was going on. Was he still asleep? He shook himself. He was cold and stiff and sore. Who did these talking rodents think he was? They were evidently afraid of him and didn't seem inclined to hurt him at all. But what if they found out he wasn't their Kingship? Lottie wasn't here to do his talking for him, so he just nodded — slightly — and stood up, saying nothing.

The lab creatures seemed very relieved. His Kingship was in a generous mood. He didn't even kick any of them! They scurried ahead, and Lewis followed up the remaining stairs with Zerox panting alongside him every step of the way.

Lewis could hear the jumbled, whispered voices that seemed to echo through the very walls of the windmill. As memories of the previous night came back to him, Lewis felt a burning knot tying itself in his gut. The NightKing's collection, Lottie had said. These voices were the stolen memories and minds of the people he had seized. And the mice — and that *rat* — must think that he, Lewis Weaver, was the NightKing. What would happen when the actual NightKing returned, as he was sure to, and soon, if they were preparing food for him? The rodents had scurried ahead and scrambled through a twisted corridor into what Lewis assumed was the tower room.

It was a round stone room with windows every few feet in the thick, cold walls. From these windows Lewis could see miles into the countryside in every direction. The sun was just rising and the horizon was pinkish gold above three green eastern hills. He had to find a way out of here. And fast. He could smell the NightKing's breakfast cooking.

There was a thick central shaft coming from the ceiling and running through the floor. This drive shaft turned when the wind blew. It led down to the gears below, which generated energy. Lewis wondered how the NightKing put the harnessed energy to work.

Lewis found it hard to concentrate with the ghostly voices bouncing off the stone all around him. It seemed much louder in this room. Why was he still here? Lottie had told him that sleep was the way home. And Lottie was gone, but he was still very much here. Between the voices bombarding him from every angle and the questions ringing through his own head, Lewis felt dizzy.

He realized that the rat was talking to him. ". . . surprised us, your Kingship," it was sniveling, "but we would know you anywhere. No matter how you transform yourself! And such a changed humor you're in, too." The ugly rat twisted his tail nervously. "You've scarcely stepped on a mouse's tail since yesterday! Ha. A-ha-ha. Ah. Ahem."

Lewis looked up and, through the gap in the ceiling, saw the massive iron machine works that held up the windmill's eight arms. The top cap of the mill turned, so that the arms could be directed toward oncoming winds.

Lewis raised his hand to his aching forehead, desperate to think of an escape. When he lifted his hand he saw the rat and mice all stoop down to the floor, cowering, shaking below him. *They think I'm going to hurt them,* Lewis thought.

He saw his chance and seized it. He scowled at the rat, raised his thick-soled field boot, and brought it down hard on the creature's ropey tail. The rat whimpered but seemed to take it in stride, almost pleased to see his Kingship back to normal. Lewis glared warningly at the mice and stomped from the room, leaving the nervous animals chattering as he rushed to find his way out.

"Serves you right, talking to him so much!"

"Oh, shut up, it didn't hurt anyway."

"Anyway, I told you it was his Kingship. . . ."

"Can *we* eat his breakfast? Shame to let it go to waste. . . ."

Lewis raced down the twisted stairs three at a time and scattered the ordinary-size, nontalking rodents as he ran. He thought at first that someone was following him, and then realized that it was Zerox. The two remembered dogs seemed determined never to lose sight of Lewis again. Without hesitating, he stumbled down the last few steps, the dogs at his side. He reached daylight and kept going, across the strange flat stones of the courtyard, out of the high walls.

He wondered if any of the creatures in the tower room would look out a window and see him running. But he couldn't stop. By the time he reached the old wall where he and Lottie had huddled the night before, he couldn't help but collapse. The dogs turned their backs to him and sat at the ends of his feet, forming a living shelter for him to cower behind. And it was just in time.

From his left he heard the increasing roar of an enormous motor and turned to see what looked like a snowmobile storming across the dry grass. Small flames sprang up in the tire tracks as sparks fell from the exhaust pipe. The strange vehicle raced toward the courtyard and the windmill. There was a very tall, thin figure hunched over the big black handlebars. A dirty lab coat flapped in the wind behind. Lewis winced at the sharp, acrid smell of burned fuel as murky smoke poured out of the reconfigured snowmobile. A black cloud of exhaust hung heavily in the air.

The NightKing was home.

And Lewis recognized his face. It was his father.

CHAPTER SIX

Blue Sparks

The next thing Lottie knew it was Monday morning and her father stood waking her up. "Schooltime, corn puff," he said. "You've had a long sleep! Slept right through Sunday! Now get yourself going, Lewis will be here any second."

Lottie gasped, remembering all over again. "Lewis," she whispered.

"What's that?" Mr. Cook asked.

"Lewis. Is, um, in Peoria. His mother called. Remember? They've gone to Peoria for a week."

Lottie gulped for air as her father, believing her tale, puttered on out of the room.

Later, at school, she had to repeat the lie several times, as everyone wondered where Lewis was. First on the walk

Betsy Pelican quizzed her relentlessly for some reason. *Why did she care?* Lottie looked nervously at Mrs. Weaver's note. It had to work. Betsy chattered on.

". . . he'll miss the spelling bee and he was on my team. Hey, that's good. . . . This way maybe we'll have a chance, since Lewis won't spell out loud and . . ."

The bell was ringing, calling them into the brick school building. The last person Lottie wanted to see was standing at the top of the steps in his usual position.

The coach stiffened but pretended not to notice Lottie as she walked up the stone steps to the school's front door. She shuddered as she walked past him. *Never mind him,* she told herself resolutely. *Rescuing Lewis is all that matters.*

She stopped to tell Mrs. Cracker, the school secretary, that Lewis was absent. For a week. Lottie stuttered her lie quickly, passed the (slightly) forged note, and made a break for it.

She headed down to Room 11 and took a deep breath as she opened the door. Everyone else was already there. Everyone else except Lewis, of course. And now she was going to have to tell her big fib in front of them, including her teacher, who could read minds.

Lottie wasn't at all sure that this was going to work. She went straight up to the front desk and fidgeted with the pencil sharpener on the corner. She had meant to keep her eyes up, looking at Ms. d'Avignon. She thought it would be more convincing. But now, no matter how she tried, her eyes kept sliding down to look at her own shoes. She was ashamed that she was lying. But what else could she do?

Ms. d'Avignon raised her eyebrows for a second as Lottie repeated the Peoria story. Lottie's heart raced, wondering if maybe Mrs. Weaver had called their teacher herself over the weekend. . . . But then the bell rang and Ms. d'Avignon was busy with other things.

Lottie didn't really hear anything in class the rest of the morning. She kept checking her pocket to make sure Lewis's notebook was there. *Lewis,* she worried to herself over and over, *Lewis, where are you?* She slumped, dazed in her chair.

When the bell rang to summon the class to P.E., Lottie sighed. Ms. d'Avignon walked them to the gym and put one hand on Lottie's shoulder as Coach Haggler approached. He had a funny look on his face when he saw her, but he blew his whistle and got back to business.

"Captains!" he barked. Brian Goode and Alan Wolf had already collected dodge balls from the bin in the corner. These two oversize twelve-year-olds had been captains of every gym class since they were six.

They pounded the hyper-inflated balls and began to choose teams. It was always exactly the same. If the game was dodgeball, Brian chose Derrick, Melanie, Betsy, Lewis, and Alice. Alan chose Eric, Scotty, Janice, Miriam, and Lottie. In that order. If the game was basketball, the order shifted a little because Derrick and Eric, the muscular twins, were very short.

Things were messed up today because Lewis was absent. Normally, when somebody was missing, Coach Haggler made the teams even by having Lottie sit out and stack sporting equipment in his office. He turned to order her in there as usual, but the snarl died on his face, as though he had reconsidered. For some reason he barked at Alice Atwell instead. Alice looked relieved actually, and she smiled almost apologetically at Lottie as she went past on her way to count balls and bats.

Brian and Alan were miffed because now Brian's team was down two players instead of just one, and that changed everything.

The game got off to a wild start, because Brian Goode couldn't remember that Lottie was on his team for a change. He pounded her twice in the head with the ball, much delighting Alan Wolf.

Lottie tried to shrug it off. She tried not to care. But her face felt hotter and hotter until steaming tears began to well up in her eyes.

Lottie had never cried at school before. She didn't cry much in general. But the dodgeball game blurred through her tears, and she didn't see the ball coming when it smacked her squarely in the nose.

She turned and ran. She ended up in the gym office with Alice Atwell, who looked startled. If anyone else noticed that Lottie had left the game, they didn't seem to mind; no one came after her.

"Are you okay, Lottie?" Alice asked.

Lottie nodded, drying her eyes on her sleeve. "I-I got hit in the face."

"Yeah." Alice seemed to understand. "It's the worst, isn't it? Dodgeball. Ugh. Except maybe SPUD. I think maybe I hate SPUD the most." Lottie and Alice looked at each other and smiled. Then suddenly they giggled.

"Will you get in trouble for being in here?" Alice asked, looking through the thick Plexiglas window at the coach, who was now keeping an eye on them.

"It doesn't matter." Lottie shrugged, taking deep breaths as her face cooled down.

"You're so, so brave, Lottie." Alice sighed as she continued stacking hockey sticks. "I'd be too afraid to do the things that you do. . . ."

Lottie knew she was usually brave. She prided herself on it. But today was different. Alice must be crazy not to notice. Didn't she see Lottie's red eyes and know that she had been crying? Crying at school! That wasn't brave.

Lottie watched Alice fumble the hockey equipment. It slid to the floor and formed an untidy pile. Alice sighed, tucked her long, straight hair behind her ears, and started again. Lottie and Alice had been in school together since first grade, but they had never become friends. They barely knew each other, really. Alice, her parents, and younger sister, Ellen, lived above their general store on Main Street. Alice worked in the store all summer and every day after school; sometimes she even left school early to help her parents. So she didn't seem to be around much. And, of course, Lottie and Lewis had usually kept to themselves anyway.

"Hey, Alice," Lottie said suddenly, "remember when you . . . um . . . interpreted Lewis's essay last week?"

Alice turned beet red and didn't even nod. Lottie fumbled in her fleecy pocket and pulled out Lewis's tiny notebook. She opened it, showing Alice the familiar squiggles. "Could you, would you look at this for me?"

Alice was red to the tips of her ears, which poked out from behind her shiny black hair. She took the notebook and looked uncertainly at Lottie. She thought perhaps Lottie might be making fun of her. But her face was serious, earnest. "It's Lewis's," Lottie said, still holding it out.

"I-I know," Alice murmured, finally taking it. "He wears it like a bracelet."

Lottie smiled. Lewis had always complained that it looked like he was wearing a bracelet. And Lottie had always told him nobody would ever think that.

Alice frowned as she turned the pages. "Why do you have it?"

"He . . . um . . . he didn't need it on his trip, and . . . um . . . he left it at my house."

"Why do you want me to read it?" Alice asked, her eyes on the page, her cheeks still bright pink. "Isn't it private?"

"I dunno. . . . I mean, he never cared if people looked, did he? And I . . . um . . . I was curious, about his . . . um . . . essay. I thought it might . . . um . . . give me ideas for mine?" Lottie felt badly about lying to Alice. She found herself holding the cherry seed tied in the corner of her pajamas and twisting it nervously.

"Oh!" Alice gasped a little, and Lottie sprang up next to her. "Look at these pages, at the end," she said nervously.

"Where?" Lottie squinted, studying the pages.

"Here." Alice showed her. "The last few pages . . . Well, first, look, all the way through the right-hand pages and the left-hand pages are mirror images of each other. . . . All of them are like that. Oh, no, not quite. Look here . . . one side is a bit different each time, here . . . and then it trails off, in a funny way. And it's a lot of the same as what he did on the chalkboard. The night, the fortress or whatever it is . . . But then here, oh, it looks terrible. Suddenly everything is out of balance. I mean, it looks like the marks want to spill off the page! Almost like they're bleeding . . ."

"Where? What does it mean?" Lottie felt the color draining from her face.

"Here it looks like his pencil lead snapped, the impression digs into the paper. It looks like a struggle and then, well . . . it's unfinished, see?"

Lottie was still looking intensely when Alice quietly closed the book. "But what does that *mean*?" Lottie demanded.

Alice shook her head. "I don't know, really. It looks awful to me. Scary. But I don't know. I don't know why I think it looks like anything. It's funny, isn't it? He never showed me his notebook before. Sometimes I saw a bit of it when other kids were looking, and somehow I always thought it, it made sense to me. I don't know why. . . ."

"No." Lottie sighed. "Neither do I." She put the little book back in her pocket and felt sadness fill her again. A struggle, bleeding, his story left unfinished . . . She shook her head. She couldn't think about that. Not now. She would go completely berserk if she thought those awful things all day. She would get Lewis back safely. She would. Somehow.

Lottie looked around the office and sighed again. She didn't feel like sorting soccer cleats. She sat down in Coach Haggler's swively armchair and pulled a couple of pencils and sheets of old paper out of the pile on the messy desk. "Let's play hangman, want to?"

Alice's brown eyes widened, and she looked nervously

out at the dodgeball game. "Can we? Should we? Won't we get in trouble?"

Lottie drew the scaffold and dashed out a long word. "Who cares?" she grumbled. Alice looked shocked, frightened, and impressed all at the same time.

"See what I mean?" She sighed at Lottie and slid nervously into the other chair. "I would never be brave enough to do what you do."

Lottie smiled in spite of herself. "Sure you would. Just guess a letter, Alice, let's play."

Before they knew it, gym class was over. They had hung each other six times, and they had become friends. Lottie walked out of the small office feeling a little stronger. *Lewis would like Alice,* she thought. And then thinking about Lewis gave her a stomachache again as they walked to their classroom to get their brown paper lunch bags.

Alice sat with her while they ate their early lunch on the hill outside the classroom. A lot of kids had to get up at the crack of dawn to milk cows or feed chickens, so the school lunch hour came quickly.

Alice was her usual quiet self, and Lottie was glad. Her mind was mostly on LightLand. She sat staring at the brick walls, chewing on her eraser instead of her lunch. When the eraser fell off, she gnawed on the bare metal end of the pencil.

The sour aluminum taste pleased her: It matched her mood. Alice was eating small, thin peanut-butter-and-onion sandwiches, like she always did. She ate three of them.

Right after lunch, Alice went home to help her parents. So for recess Lottie sat swaying on a swing by herself. It was a beautiful fall day. The clouds were round and high and bright against the blue sky. Lottie didn't notice.

She held Lewis's notebook tightly in her hand. Was it some kind of message, a clue? She took it out and looked at it until her head hurt from trying to understand the squiggles. She kept hearing Umber's words in her mind, "You don't need to *try*. . . ." How could she help but try?

"What's going on, Charlotte?"

Lottie fell clean off the swing, startled by Ms. d'Avignon's voice. The other sixth graders cleared out.

"Huh? Nothing, I'm just . . . um." Lottie tried to regain some composure and climbed back on the swing. "Nothing." She smiled weakly at her teacher.

"So," Ms. d'Avignon continued. "Lewis is still *away*."

"Peoria. His aunt. She lives there. It was last minute." Lottie could feel her face flush bright red.

"Right, you mentioned that yesterday. I was just wondering when you'd tell me where he really was."

Lottie stared. She froze for a moment, panicking. Then she nervously twisted the swing, turning herself in a tight circle.

"Charlotte, I *would* like to know where Lewis is. I expect you to tell me."

Ms. d'Avignon walked away, her shoulder-length hair swirling in the breeze. Lottie lifted her feet and went into a wild spin, the chains of the swing unwinding and winding again as the momentum gradually gave out.

When the three o'clock bell finally rang, and the students gathered their backpacks to go home, Ms. d'Avignon asked Lottie to stay after class a minute. Lottie swallowed hard and sat back down.

Brian Goode chuckled and nudged Alan Wolf. They loved to see someone get in trouble. This was great! They tried to linger in the doorway to hear what was going on, but their teacher shooed them out. Lottie didn't care about them, but she put her head down flat on her desk.

She wondered what she was supposed to tell her teacher. Surely not the truth. It's hard to imagine saying something like, "You want to know the honest truth about Lewis? He has vanished into another world altogether. Where? Why it's in a small wooden shoe box tucked under my pillow, of course. And by the way, for all I know, he may never return." Lottie shivered and closed her eyes as the classroom emptied.

"Well!" Ms. d'Avignon sat at her desk with a tired smile on her face. "Are you ready to talk?"

Lottie nodded, and tried to smile, but really she just looked sick to her stomach.

"I'm concerned, Charlotte."

Lottie felt in her heart that it was useless to lie. Her teacher could look right through her and know what was in her mind. But the truth was too sticky, too difficult to explain.

She stared guiltily at her shoes and said nothing.

"I see." Ms. d'Avignon looked sad. "Why don't I walk home with you?"

Lottie silently walked the long way home, around the edge of the cornfield, with Ms. d'Avignon at her side. She felt herself sinking into despair. *Without Lewis what difference did anything make? If she ever got back into LightLand, she'd find a way to stay there with him forever. . . .*

"Cheer up, Charlotte," Ms. d'Avignon said quietly as they finally turned down Lottie's gravel driveway. "It's never as bleak as all that. Running away is never the answer."

Lottie hardly noticed that her teacher had read her mind again. Maybe she was getting used to it. Or maybe she was too depressed to care. They walked past the towering line of sunflowers she had planted months earlier, the massive seed heads bowing slightly to the dozens of field birds that feasted there. They climbed the sagging porch steps to the

Cooks' house, and Lottie's father came through the screen door to greet them.

Lottie never forgot the next moment as long as she lived. Every detail seemed to stand out even then, and the world turned in slow motion. . . .

Her father, dressed in his dusty, blue coveralls, had been building something. He held a hammer in his left hand as he stretched out his right hand to meet Ms. d'Avignon. There was a nail between his teeth and it glinted in the afternoon sun as he smiled. His faded blue eyes twinkled as they almost always did.

Ms. d'Avignon, in her long, pale yellow school dress, looked as fresh and soft as this morning's corn silk, smiling up the steps at him. She had a curious look in her sharp green eyes as she stretched out her hand.

And when Eldon Cook's long thin fingers met Margo d'Avignon's lovely tapered fingers blue sparks crackled from their hands.

Lottie seemed to be the only one to notice the sparks, which tumbled off their handshake and popped around their feet for a second before they disappeared. The handshake lasted just a fraction of a second longer than necessary, and then Mr. Cook invited everyone to come in for a nice glass of lemonade.

CHAPTER SEVEN

A Small New Friend

Lewis and Zerox were huddled in the shrubbery, looking at the windmill through a dirty haze of exhaust smoke.

The NightKing was his father.

There was no doubt about it. Lewis had seen his face quite clearly and all his early memories played through his head. This was the same man. The distant look in his eyes that Lewis remembered had changed into an icy, piercing glare. The somber face now had a cruel sneer plastered across it. It was mottled by ugly scars. But it was the same man.

How is it possible? How did it happen? That day, long ago, when his father had disappeared from Iowa, this must be where he had gone. And now he was the NightKing, a living nightmare. He prowled at night, terrorizing everyone in

LightLand. *And he is my father* . . . Lewis thought with a wave of nausea.

Lewis felt his head reeling. His hands trembled and his stomach tied itself into a hard knot. What did this mean about his own future? If his father had never returned, would Lewis ever be able to escape? Was he trapped in LightLand forever?

They said that the NightKing had no story of his own, but Lewis knew that wasn't true. He remembered much of his father's story. He remembered things that his grandparents had told him. . . . Things Lewis himself had done with his father as a little boy. Had those memories vanished in his father's twisted mind?

The deep marks grooved into the paving stones, the matching marks in Lewis's notebook — what was the link between the two of them? Was this his destiny, like Alice Atwell had said?

Lewis stood up and ran. He ran farther than ever before. He wanted to get away, as far away as possible. The dogs loped alongside him, panting. Finally Lewis collapsed in exhaustion. His sides ached; his heart was pounding.

He could no longer see the windmill. Breathing deeply, he tried to think what to do next.

One of the dogs, perhaps sensing Lewis's sadness, licked his hand and nuzzled its soft head against his arm. He was grateful for the company. The bushes behind him were scratchy, and Lewis now saw that they were berry bushes. Blackcaps! They were his favorite. He stuffed himself on the berries and remembered that he'd eaten nothing since dinner at Lottie's house, which seemed like a thousand years ago. When the berries were depleted, he was still hungry, but certainly he was much better off than he had been.

You would think that eating something would have improved Lewis's outlook. Actually, it was just the opposite. Now that his stomach was no longer growling, his brain felt free to completely focus on the larger problem. As he sat rubbing the berry juice from his hands, Lewis sank deeper into despair.

He felt as though he couldn't move. He was so confused, so miserable, that he just sat, staring at the ground. He could see worn, smokey paths where his father, the Night-King, must have ridden. Some of the small fires that had flared up in the path were still burning. Lewis didn't notice at first that a smallish, ordinary-looking brown mouse was watching him from a comfortable distance. In fact, he was staring right at the small creature without seeing it. The mouse was a blurry part of the background until Lewis realized that it was waving at him.

A little paw was timidly waving as it nodded its small head up and down nervously.

Lewis waved back a little bit. He felt foolish, but the mouse was delighted and bobbed its head enthusiastically. Bowing, the creature took a few steps backward. Lewis sat up. The Zerox dogs raised their heads and saw the mouse, but they didn't seem to mind it.

Lewis turned his head to the side, thinking, watching the mouse. It was dancing nervously, forward and backward, bobbing its head encouragingly. Lewis crouched on his feet, towering over the tiny animal. The dogs looked at Lewis and seemed to await his next move. The mouse beckoned with its paw, whiskers twitching. Lewis scratched his head. Anything was possible, it seemed.

The mouse looked at him pleadingly. Lewis shook himself a little to be sure he was seeing things clearly. He was. *Well,* he thought, *I can hide here in the weeds for the rest of my life, or I can try something else.* He took a deep breath and decided to follow the mouse, which was clearly what the animal wanted.

It's probably one of the NightKing's servants, Lewis thought as he moved. *One of the rodents from the lab. He sent them out to find me and lure me back, I suppose. I can't just sit here,* he thought. *I've got no better ideas of my own, so I may as well follow.*

Lewis thought somehow that this mouse had a nice face.

On a small, ordinary mousey scale, he had an earnest, trust-worthy face. And Lewis followed him.

At one point the mouse led him past a smoldering pit where there had been a fire very recently. There was a horri-ble smell billowing out in smokey gusts that were carried on the wind. The smell made Lewis feel ill. If he'd had more in his stomach, he probably would've thrown up. The mouse veered wildly to avoid the pit and put considerable distance between the smell and themselves before returning to the path they were following.

Lewis looked cautiously around. He could still see the three hills that he'd noticed from the windmill. The vegeta-tion around them was sparse and scruffy, and just beyond the random clumps of bushes Lewis saw images.

His early memories played out around him just as they had for Lottie. But where Lottie had seen scattered visions of a happy childhood, Lewis saw glimpses of the father he had almost forgotten.

Then the mouse abruptly stopped.

Nodding, the mouse seemed to be pointing downward. Suddenly he vanished into the ground and then, just as sud-denly, reappeared. Lewis stared as he did it again, pointing dramatically. Lewis understood and nodded back. The mouse had led him to some sort of secret trench that was covered entirely by thick weeds at the top. Lewis would never have found it on his own.

The mouse slid between the weeds again, his little paw protruding and beckoning. Lewis prodded the spot with his boot, careful not to squash his guide. The weeds seemed to have nothing below them at all. Lewis sat at what turned out to be the edge and eased both his feet through. His ankles disappeared, his legs, and then, holding the top weeds in his fists, Lewis went through entirely.

He found himself at the top of a very steep, narrow, rocky ravine. It seemed to go on forever: forward, backward, and down. A strange lattice of light filtered through the lid of grass. Lewis thought with a shudder that he was glad he hadn't walked this way on his own and fallen down here without seeing the trench first. He would certainly have broken his neck.

The mouse gave a faint squeak, flopped on his belly, and began to slide downward. The twin dogs had poked their heads through, but whimpered unhappily. They couldn't make a descent like this. Lewis rubbed their ears gently. *I'll be back,* he tried to tell them with his eyes. *Don't worry, you won't lose me again.*

The dogs seemed to understand perfectly well. They licked Lewis affectionately on the cheek, whimpered a last time, and pulled their heads back out through the grass, disappearing.

The mouse gave a squeak from far below that echoed up the sides of the ravine. With another deep breath, Lewis sat clumsily and slid down the rocky slide, careful not to overtake and squish the mouse.

By the time they reached the end of the rock slide, Lewis was extremely sore and truly terrified. He was chilled throughout, and his hands shook again with fear. The bottom of the ravine was mucky and smelly. Lewis couldn't seem to breathe properly. He couldn't gulp enough air.

He got quickly to his feet and found he could easily touch the walls on both sides of the trench. He was kicking himself for being led into what must surely be a trap. Gasping furiously for enough air, Lewis peered at the mouse and suddenly thought — though how could one be sure? — that the mouse was terrified, too.

Seeing the shaking mouse at his feet, the icy feeling inside Lewis began to melt. A very tiny thread of hope connected him to the frightened mouse.

With a shudder of resignation, he walked hunched over behind the scurrying mouse. They walked for hours, silently. It was very slow progress, due to the trickling water, the slippery rocks, the logistics of trying to let a mouse lead. Lewis had lost all sense of direction. He hit his head hard several times on juttings of rock and earth. Of course, he mostly assumed now that he was being led back the way they had come. In his despair, he assumed he was marching directly into the torture chamber of the NightKing.

In a way, he was.

The trench gradually became a tunnel. Murky, stinky water trickled through the bottom. Lewis's socks and leather boots were soon wet all the way through. The air filled with a greenish glow that was the same eerie light he had seen inside the windmill the night before. Somewhere far above him he was sure he heard the groan of the windmill blades. His heart sank even lower, but he followed all the same. In the dim light, his little leader squeaked occasionally so that Lewis could be sure of the direction.

Lewis still thought about turning back, but honestly, he didn't see how that would help him. He might as well go forward as back.

They began to hear scratchy, whispery sounds in the ceiling above their heads. The rats. Other mice. Scurrying above them. The little guide mouse looked back at Lewis and rolled his eyes upward as though to say, Do you hear the others? Lewis nodded and realized that in this very mousey, rattish tunnel he had not yet seen another rodent at all. That was either a good sign or it was suspicious. He took a deep breath and gave his full trust over to his little new friend.

Everything changed then. Oh, they were still making their way through a smelly, disgusting tunnel; they were still marching to near certain doom, but they were doing it together. Lewis's mood brightened considerably. Trusting his fate to the small, vulnerable mouse, believing in the wisdom of his new, true companion, gave him strength.

"Friend?"

Lewis heard the voice and realized that his tiny guide was talking to him. Lewis was startled, but nodded.

"Above he is. The one you seek." The mouse nodded.

What did it mean? Lewis wasn't *seeking* the NightKing. He wanted to get as far away from him as possible.

Didn't he?

But the mouse kept nodding, and said again, "The one you seek . . ." trying to show that it understood Lewis's mind. And something happened. Lewis nodded, too. He realized with strange certainty that he was, indeed, seeking his father. The mouse was right. He wanted to find him, to face him. His fear of the NightKing began to be transformed until Lewis actually felt that he was looking forward to meeting him again.

He, Lewis Weaver, was here for a reason. He was the one who could change the world. He could reach something good somewhere deep inside the man who had been married to his mother. Amazed at himself, he smiled in the dark and moved more quickly.

"Look for the Veil first," the mouse squeaked cautiously.

Lewis cocked his head, puzzled.

"I will help you search for it, but the danger will be great."

Lewis didn't understand. His shook his head, confused.

"The Veil. The dark Veil. The Veil of Oblivion," the mouse was still nodding. It looked surprised that Lewis didn't understand. "The NightKing wraps sleepers in the Veil, until their eyes are blank."

Lewis furrowed his brow, remembering what Lottie had been told. He thought of the voices echoing in the windmill, the stolen memories.

"Yes," the mouse nodded seriously. "Without the Veil, we think he will be weak."

Lewis shook his head quickly to clear his thoughts. This couldn't be a job for him. This was Lottie's mission, maybe. She was the brave one.

"Your heart. Your mind. We use these for power. We must destroy the Veil."

Somehow Lewis found himself nodding, though he had no idea how he would do any of these things.

"But you must find the right one . . ." the mouse continued.

Lewis frowned but followed as the two began clawing their way up the slippery rock wall face.

"There are many." The mouse's small voice was barely a whisper now.

Lewis had to strain to hear the tiny voice of his companion. The sound came trickling back to him like water dripping and splashing here and there against the rocks.

"He trusts not even his rats. He has made many Veils, to prevent them from stealing. We must be careful, take only the right one. The wrong ones hold other dangers."

The mouse stopped speaking as they reached a wide, round space carved out of the rock wall. The mouse scurried into it and Lewis followed, surprised to find that there was room enough for him. He couldn't sit up quite straight, but if he slumped against the wall, he was amazingly comfortable.

"We'll rest here for the night," whispered the mouse.

Lewis was astounded. He had such adrenaline rushing through him, he couldn't imagine sleeping. He shook his head.

"Listen," the mouse chirped. Somewhere far away, a bell was sounding. "It only tolls at midnight."

Lewis couldn't believe the time. They had hiked all day. He had taken no rest at all. And he hadn't eaten anything but the blackcap berries since the night at Lottie's. His stomach growled loudly at the memory. The hungry rumbling seemed extraordinarily loud in the small cave. The mouse smiled broadly.

"Hideaway. Carved out by the True Mice." He was proud. "It fits you."

Lewis nodded, smiling, leaning back again. Suddenly his muscles gave out. He was tired, after all.

His friend was pleased. "I am a True Mouse, called October. I watched you, last night, entering the fortress. I knew you would help us."

Lewis nodded at October, glad to know his name. He almost spoke to say his own name, but found he couldn't. He wished that Lottie were there to speak for him, like she had his whole life.

"Sleep now. Tomorrow, there will be no rest!" October the True Mouse curled into a ball against Lewis's leg. Lewis had to smile. It was almost cozy. He didn't close his eyes, of course, but he did sleep. He slept all night.

When Lewis awoke hours later, it was to a small scratchy feeling on his hand. October the True Mouse was sitting on his palm, looking at him with a strange expression on his face.

Lewis returned the quizzical look.

"It's true," October whispered, "what they say about your eyes. You *don't* sleep. Like him." The mouse just stared, his whiskers twitching.

Lewis yawned and shook his head gently. Of course he slept. He'd been sleeping right up to that moment.

October was unconvinced. He seemed more reverential somehow, now that he had seen the way Lewis slept. He scurried to the edge of the small cave and peered upward. "We should move now. This is the time."

Lewis hated the thought of moving. He was surprisingly well rested, but he ached so from the long trek the day before. He began to move and then sank back into the wall of the cave again with a heavy sigh.

"We *must* move now. And silently," October insisted.

Lewis nodded and rolled to the edge. The mouse scrambled quickly upward. It was painful for Lewis, unfolding his legs and arms until they protruded from the small round cave. He felt a shiver of excitement run through his veins, however, as he pulled himself up and out.

What would the day bring?

He and October climbed silently. The space narrowed, the air changed and it occurred to Lewis that something was quite different now. *Were they climbing through the thick walls of the windmill itself?* He found it hard to breathe and tried to remain calm as he climbed on and on. Then suddenly he thought that he heard activity on the other side of the stone. Yes, there it was again. He could hear something.

He tapped quietly on the wall, getting the mouse's attention. He tapped and pointed to the stone.

"Shhh." October was barely audible, mouthing the words. "No more now, friend. Silence only."

Lewis wanted to know what the sounds were; he wanted

121

to know where he was. He tapped once more, insistently, and a small rock chip dislodged, falling with a clattering sound far, far below them.

"Or perish!" the mouse whispered harshly, and they climbed on higher and higher in silence until they could see the stone close off above them.

October led him up underneath the ledge ceiling, and then Lewis could see a greenish, glowing crack in the rock. It illuminated their faces more clearly and Lewis saw that the mouse was waiting for him to act. The crack was large enough for October, and he disappeared and reappeared through it several times, just as he had done at the hidden edge of the ravine. But where was the hidden way in for Lewis this time?

October showed him, pretending to push on the edge of the crack, as though it were a sliding door that could be moved aside. Lewis pushed with all his might against the crack but nothing happened. There was still only a spot wide enough for a mouse to slip through. Nothing bigger than Lewis's nose was going to get by. October was gesturing frantically.

The mouse pointed at his head, thumped his own little chest, clutched at his heart, nodding and pointing, and then, somehow, Lewis understood. His heart and his mind. He had to believe first that he could do it and then he could do it. He had to know that it would happen and then it would happen.

He took a deep breath. He imagined himself climbing through the passage. He would be able to do it, he told himself, because he had to be able to do it. The passage *would* widen because he needed it to widen.

And it did.

This time, with the lightest touch, the crack became wider and wider. The two comrades easily passed through, and as soon as they did, the crack closed again silently.

Lewis blinked. They were high above ground level. He felt certain of it, though there were no windows, no natural light. The crack in the stone had sealed behind them tightly, and October patted it, shaking his head at Lewis. They couldn't get back out that way.

The greenish glow of the room they had entered seemed unbearably bright. His head ached suddenly with the glare of it and he blinked thickly several times, confused by what he saw. After so long underground, this room made his eyes throb. Lewis's vision adjusted and he took a deep breath, steeling himself for what was to come.

The windowless room they had slipped into was dirty and smelled of mildew. Lewis tried not to despair when he realized that the stone chamber was filled with thousands and thousands of lengths of cloth . . . sacks and bags of every shape and size.

There were flour sacks and sewn leather bags, twine ropes, silk and satin sheets, sacks made of metal mesh, and sacks of heavy tapestry. They were plain, fancy, old, and new. Some were filthy, some pristine. He turned to look behind him. And there, reclined in the middle of this pile, was his father.

There was no mistaking the identity of the man in front of them. It wasn't like looking into a mirror or anything, but there could be no doubt. Lewis felt a wave of deep cold fear wash over him as he looked at the rough, scarred face.

The NightKing was looking right at him, staring. His gray eyes blinked normally but his head was tilted downward and his mouth was relaxed. This appearance had been described to Lewis many times by Lottie, and he knew just what it meant.

The NightKing was asleep.

CHAPTER EIGHT

Solid Memories

Though she didn't see any more blue sparks, Lottie couldn't take her eyes off Ms. d'Avignon as they sat around the kitchen table. Neither could her father. The soft-spoken teacher, however, let her eyes wander all around the room, absorbing every little detail.

She glimpsed the end of the crooked hall that seemed to have more doors than was possible leading from it. She looked out the window and saw the kitchen fields that grew just enough produce for the two Cooks, plus usually Lewis. She noticed the sunlight bending softly through the windows. The light bounced off a collection of different plaques and mementos that hung on the walls. There were dozens of black-and-white photographs in tarnished frames. There was one of a tall man in a military uniform. He looked so authoritative, so independent, so much like Lottie, that Ms. d'Avignon almost laughed out loud. She smiled instead.

While Eldon poured icy lemonade into blue Mason jars, Ms. d'Avignon asked again about Lewis.

At the mention of Lewis's name, Lottie turned pale. The kitchen suddenly felt unbearably stuffy. She bit her lip and looked at the adults. Ms. d'Avignon was staring at her, waiting. Lottie glanced away.

Her father didn't seem to understand. "Lewis?"

"Yes, *Lewis* . . ." the teacher said softly and kept her eyes on Lottie, who was nervously gripping her hands together.

Mr. Cook was puzzled. "Lewis had to go to Peoria with his —" When he saw the guilty look on his daughter's face, he stopped. "Or — is he somewhere else?" Lottie couldn't lie again. She nodded.

She was surprised by how relieved she felt with just that one nod. She could breathe again. The two grown-ups simply sat in their chairs and waited. They didn't scold or threaten her, but they were waiting. Lottie didn't know how to begin and didn't know how to begin and still didn't know how to begin. Until she began.

After many cups of her father's icy lemonade and after much thoughtful consideration of Ms. d'Avignon's strange, shadowy eyes, Lottie decided to tell them.

Everything.

She brought the StoryBox to the kitchen and hugged it to her chest while she told them. At first she expected them to laugh at her, and she looked into the box and fidgeted with her fingers while she spoke. She was sure it was a mistake to tell grown-ups, even these grown-ups, anything like this. All children know adults only believe what they want to believe. Lottie waited for them to tell her she was dreaming, imagining.

But what Lottie learned that day, and what changed her view of the world in many ways, is that some grown-ups *are* different. Some can be trusted. Some will believe.

When she finished telling about Lewis, about the box, the tree, the NightKing . . . she heard her father's deep, contented sigh. He reached for the StoryBox carefully, patting the lid with a certain proud, thoughtful touch.

Ms. d'Avignon had moved to the edge of the back door and stood staring out in the direction where the cherry tree used to stand. Both of these adults had an unusual look in their eyes. It was a glimmer that Lottie was sure she had seen before, but now, suddenly, it surprised her. She had never noticed that look in an *adult's* eyes before.

"Fantastic . . ." Ms. d'Avignon murmured under her breath. "I think I knew it. . . . I was really almost sure of it. . . ."

"You believe me, then?" Lottie asked in a quavering voice.

"Oh, yes!" Ms. d'Avignon replied, still staring outside. "Of course, it has been a very, very long time. LightLand . . . I was eleven years old as well!"

Lottie was stunned. "But-but-but —" She was unnerved. "How can you know about LightLand?"

She turned to look at her father. He was watching the teacher with mild, pleased surprise, but he certainly was not *stunned*. And he nodded. "Yes, LightLand," he agreed. "I was twelve."

"You've both been there?" Lottie was incredulous. "Has *everyone* been there?!"

"No, no, not at all." Her father smiled. "Your teacher here is only the fourth person I ever met — you and Lewis would be second and third."

"There are very few people in our world who discover the power of their memories," Ms. d'Avignon went on, "like you have. And Lewis. And for you the links between the worlds may sometimes open. . . ."

"And for you?" Lottie interrupted.

"Yes." Ms. d'Avignon nodded. "And for your father. The box is wonderful, Eldon. How did you think of it?"

"Oh, it just seemed right at the time," Mr. Cook replied, almost blushing. *My father never blushes,* Lottie thought, frowning, and stared at them.

"If you've never seen the box how can you know about

LightLand?" she demanded of her teacher. "LightLand is *in* the StoryBox, isn't it?"

"In the StoryBox?" Her father sounded puzzled. "There are any number of ways there, ways *in,* as you say. But the box was, well, my own idea."

Ms. d'Avignon nodded appreciatively. "The StoryBox is perfect as a bridge to LightLand. The cherry wood must be powerful because it spans important memories. . . . Yours and your mother's."

Eldon smiled. "And mine," he added.

Lottie's head was spinning. She couldn't begin to understand what they were talking about. "Are you saying that LightLand is just, just memories? Not real? Because that can't be true —"

"*Just* memories!" Ms. d'Avignon seemed to realize there was teaching to be done. "No! Certainly not! You're completely correct: LightLand is real. LightLand is every bit as real as it is different from our own world. But there are links between the two places. Magical links, you might say. Old stories and bits of memory that might otherwise be lost are often the touchstone.

"A dark side has always existed there — plenty of memories are terrible, after all. *Nunc Lux, Munc Nox —*"

Lottie stared and recited, " 'Now it is Light, suddenly it is Night' . . . I didn't understand before."

"Yes." Her father nodded. "The battle between remembering and forgetting is like the one between day and night. It is LightLand's greatest struggle."

"Do you think Lewis is all right?" Lottie asked in a whisper. "Is it safe?"

"No, it isn't safe. It's an adventure. There's no such thing as a safe adventure, Charlotte." Ms. d'Avignon shook her head, and Lottie turned pale once again.

"You'll have to go get him," her father said firmly, and Ms. d'Avignon agreed.

"You've got to go back at once. Even if you can't bring him back this time, try to find out just what's going on. Find out why it is different for Lewis."

Lottie put her hands on her head to try to control the spinning feeling. "But I've *tried*. Weren't you listening? I've tried for three days and I *can't*. I don't know how!" Lottie was red in the face suddenly and her lower lip was trembling. Her father put his arms around her, forming a small safe circle. He pressed the magic box into her hands.

"You can," he said quietly. "Because you must. That's all you need to know." Something in her mind sharpened. She felt as though the cutting little edges of a crystal had begun to form there. She was sensing, though she didn't realize it yet, that everything was possible. It would require a bit of magic, perhaps, but it was possible. She took the lid off the box.

"I can," she repeated, "because I have to. . . ."

"Think of a memory, Charlotte. You have them all available now."

Lottie wrinkled her forehead and bit her lip.

"Tell an old story that might help you. Sometimes old ones are best. And remember, it may be there when you get there," her father added.

Be there when you get there? Lottie thought of the visions she'd seen, and of Zerox, the identical dogs. Lewis remembered them and they came. That strange wobbly feeling rushed through her. There were difficult memories fighting to come to the front of her mind. Her hands shook again like they had that night in LightLand. What was wrong with her? Ms. d'Avignon was watching her curiously.

Lottie tried to clear her head. She needed to focus on helping Lewis now. Anything else could wait. What should she remember that might be helpful? Her eyes fell on the black-and-white photograph of the soldier hanging on the wall.

"I remember," Lottie began quietly, closing her eyes, wrapping her mind around a story. "I remember Grandpa Reeder. I have some of his medals, stars, and badges in my top dresser drawer. I always wanted to be more like him. . . ."

Lottie hesitated, opened her eyes, and stared down into the now glowing cherry wood box. She closed her eyes again and tried to see the story in her head as clearly as possible, wondering if this would work, if it would get her back to LightLand. She thought to herself that this story was a good choice. Remembering a war hero. If he appeared like Zerox had, he would be a big help! She tried to picture what he had looked like, what she had been told. . . .

"He had red hair and freckles and ears like jug handles. When he was a kid he swam every summer in a rocky swimming hole in Maine. The water was icy, even in August.

"One time another kid, who didn't know the shallow spots, dove in and hit the rocks. He knocked himself out cold and disappeared under the freezing water. My great-grandmother said, 'Russell, go get him.'

"So he kicked off his shoes and dove after the boy. He still had on his jacket and knickers. The lake was deep and dark and icy cold. But he swam down until he felt the lumpy top of the boy's head and pulled him up by the hair. And saved him." Lottie smiled, imagining how he must have looked.

"He won his first medal for that. He was fourteen, if the story is true," Lottie finished.

"Yeah, that's true, pretty much," said a voice she didn't quite recognize.

Lottie about jumped out of her skin when she turned around and saw the gangly redheaded boy. He had ears that stood out from the sides of his head. Freckles swirled over his cheeks. He was more than a shadowy vision. However, he didn't seem completely real either. He was somewhere between solid and merely remembered. When he looked at Lottie, he grinned ear to ear, his eyes disappearing into his smile.

"Hello there." He was laughing at her, a loud, deep laugh. "What the heck are you *wearing*?" Lottie, in her fleecy pajamas, was quite a contrast to his tweed jacket and knickers that drooped from his shoulders to his knobbly knees.

Lottie squinted in the bright sunlight. She remembered to smile and she said hello. She looked around quickly. She wasn't in her kitchen anymore. Her father and Ms. d'Avignon were nowhere to be seen. She was back in LightLand.

"I'm Russell."

Lottie stood there stupidly. She couldn't call him Russell. However, *Grandpa* clearly wasn't going to work either.

"You can call me Red if you want to," the boy said, pointing to his bright hair as if in explanation.

"Right. I've . . . um . . . I've heard of you," Lottie stuttered, still staring with her mouth hanging open.

Red seemed pleased. "Did you see me play first base?"

Lottie smiled, liking him. "No, I . . . um . . . I heard about your medals. You're a hero. . . ."

Red's ears wiggled. "Awww, I just did what my mother told me," he said.

"But then the war! All the medals you won —" Lottie

started but stopped suddenly. She understood. Those other medals hadn't happened yet. *This* Russell Reeder was fourteen years old, still fifteen years away from all that other stuff. Twenty years away from being her mother's father.

Red surveyed the field. "Say, where is this place?"

Lottie mumbled a semi-explanation, which — amazingly — seemed to satisfy Red. She just told him that her friend Lewis was lost. Red nodded and looked around, getting his bearings.

As overwhelmed as she was to meet him, deep down Lottie was disappointed. What good would a fourteen-year-old be? Well, at least she was back in LightLand.

"Let's walk around, figure out where we are. I'll find your friend, no trouble," he said, rubbing his hands together.

Lottie wished that she were as optimistic as the young Red Reeder. But she didn't see anything she recognized: no windmill, no stone wall, no cherry tree. Just rolling fields and fields and fields of corn. How was she going to find Lewis?

The corn looked almost like an ocean, swelling up and down. The wind was mild and just ruffled the tops of the stalks as it rolled along the waves. Red took off striding through the rows before he'd even finished talking. He might not be a commander yet, but he sure wasn't much for just sitting and thinking things over, Lottie noticed as she ran along behind him through the tall corn.

This was her third trip to LightLand. She ought to be able to get her bearings, but it all looked unfamiliar to her. What had Umber said? *Never the same way twice.*

Lottie almost had to gallop to keep up with her young, long-legged grandfather. He whistled and squinted in the bright morning sunlight, and he asked Lottie questions about herself. "You sure do remind me of somebody," Red kept saying, shaking his head. He couldn't quite put his finger on it. . . .

"I know what you mean," Lottie agreed. He distracted her from her panic. She found that she couldn't stare hard enough at his smile, his freckles, and the take-charge look in his eyes. It was like having a little bit of her mother walking around with her. But when the sun hit him full on, his outline shimmered, as though he would vanish any second. She fought off a desire to hold his hand.

"I wonder how I got here?" Red scratched his head. Lottie just shrugged. "Last thing I knew, it was past ten and my mother was yelling for me to go to bed. Now here I am with you and it's barely midmorning."

Lottie felt this nervous fluttering worry that he was going to evaporate. What if this was her only chance ever to know him?

He sure liked talking about himself, and Lottie was grateful. He loved sports, dogs, and train rides. Dreamed about getting a real automobile someday, if his mother would let him. Planned to be a baseball player when he grew up. Had so many things he wanted to do, he didn't think he'd ever have time to get married.

Lottie smiled. She remembered the story of what would happen next in his life. Of the girl he would meet in a few years who would be sitting on a piano stool, twisting her long brown braids. That would be Dort, and he would marry her. She would be Lottie's grandmother.

"I guess you never know," she said.

He taught Lottie his favorite song, and they walked along singing, *"Camp town ladies sing this song, doo-dah, doo-dah —"*

Red squinted into the distance. "There's a line of trees, that way."

Lottie looked and saw nothing but corn.

"Maybe there's something to see on the other side. Let's go." Red was moving before he'd finished speaking, weaving his way among the rows as though he'd done it all his life.

Lottie, who *had* done it all her life, tried to hurry and ended up losing a slipper when she tripped over a heavy clod of dirt. Red moved so fast on his long legs that he had just about reached the trees by the time Lottie had her slipper back on. She lost sight of him. Where was he? Running along after him, Lottie called his name, and she thought she heard him laughing his loud booming laugh. Then she heard something else.

"*Squawk!* Lottie Cook!"

"Umber!" Lottie was breathless with relief. She emerged from the corn and found the bird fluttering through some scrawny pine trees. But Red was nowhere to be seen.

"Where — where did my grandfather go?"

Umber landed on a branch at eye level. "Bygones. Hard to hold. Solid memories are rare."

"I wasn't done with him! Where is he?"

Umber whistled. "Gone. Back to your memory."

"*You're* real, you're solid and you came from my memory, didn't you? How did I make you?"

The bird puffed up. "Solid memories in LightLand are its citizens. No one asks How of us. No one asks Why of us." Then, almost shyly, he added, "Perhaps I am not *your* memory. Your father built the StoryBox. Years ago, he remembered. And years are long in LightLand. He remembered me. I waited. For you."

Lottie's eyes widened as she thought this over. "But my grandfather . . . I wish I could have made him real. I was just getting to know him!"

"*Squawk.* Look inside, Lottie Cook."

Lottie looked inside herself. She expected to feel sad,

devastated really. But she didn't. The memory of her grandfather was so strong now; it was as though she was carrying
him around within. She *remembered* him. And she knew she
would never forget him. His determination pounded inside
her own chest and reminded her of her real mission. She had
to find Lewis.

"I shouldn't waste the daylight this time. We need to find
him right away. Have you seen him?" Lottie asked, and Umber
swooned.

"Seen him?! Seen the NightKing? Lottie Cook, I couldn't
fly here talking to you if I had seen the NightKing! I'd be a
bygone thing for certain."

"No, no, not the NightKing," Lottie frowned. "*Lewis.*
I'm here to rescue Lewis."

"Ahhh. It appears that they are one and the same. Their
eyes. The Lewis doesn't sleep . . . he cannot escape. The
NightKing, *the Lewis.* You see?"

"Can't escape?" Lottie seethed. "He is too going to escape. That's what I'm here for. You can go your own way for
all I care. I'm here for Lewis!"

Umber fluffed his feathers and spoke as slowly as he
knew how. "The Lewis —"

"Stop calling him that! He's not *the* Lewis; he's *my*
Lewis!" Lottie snarled.

Umber's feathers ruffled. "*Your* Lewis, then. Dreams are

the only way home, and your Lewis doesn't sleep. In Light-Land there is only one other like that. The NightKing —"

"Lewis sleeps!" Lottie interrupted. "He just sleeps with his eyes open! That doesn't make him your stupid NightKing."

"All the same," Umber insisted. "The NightKing is not pleased about your Lewis. The mice heard his name, Lottie, as well as yours. The NightKing sees you coming. But now there's a long day ahead! And we can move freely. We can seize the Veil."

Lottie scowled. "Is Lewis still — is he okay?"

"If your Lewis had been Veiled, we would have found him outside." Umber shrugged his feathers.

"What if we *do* find him like that?" Lottie's heart pounded. "Like Robert?"

Umber's feathers puffed and ruffled. "Either Veiled. Or he is on the wrong side. Either."

Lottie was furious.

"Lewis is *not* on the wrong side!" she howled. "Don't ever say that again."

The bird was unconvinced. "Prisoner, perhaps," he whistled skeptically. "The NightKing will never let you take him home. Break his power first."

Lottie swallowed hard as she realized that Umber was right. At last she nodded. Umber squawked.

* * *

The bird had a plan.

There didn't seem to be much to it, in Lottie's opinion. It revolved around the basic idea that Lottie would challenge the NightKing face-to-face. Umber thought she should go at once, by day, when his dominance seemed less. She would destroy the powerful Veil of Oblivion, whatever it was. Umber seemed sure that Lottie was the one to do this. That her temperament and memory and stories might be all she would need.

"By day he is in his fortress, not seeing, not stirring. You, Lottie Cook, must find the Veil of Oblivion by day," Umber insisted as they walked.

"I don't understand."

"Without it, we hope, the NightKing will have no power. Lottie Cook must defeat the Veil!"

"What makes you think I can do that?"

"Years, I told them. Lottie Cook, I said! Lottie Cook must try, today." Umber nodded. "We read the signs."

"I haven't seen any signs," Lottie grumbled.

Umber whistled at her. "Cherry tree! First sign! Smoke, lights! You! All signs. We listen to the fortress, we hear many things."

The fortress was evidently the windmill, where Lottie had left Lewis asleep on the spiraling stairs. She was happy to be heading straight for it, though she wasn't looking forward to hearing the disembodied voices again. She looked for courage deep inside and had to smile when she discovered the memory of her grandfather was still there. He was brave. And so was she. She sang his song as she walked, *"Gwine to run all night, Gwine to run all day, I'll bet my money on the bob-tail nag, Somebody bet on the bay."*

A great surprise was waiting for her leaning against an oak tree at a bend in the path. Blinking in the sunlight and struggling to stay awake was a gangly yellow-haired boy. A brown cat waited with him.

"Robert!" Lottie called out in surprise.

"Right. I'm Robert." The boy nodded, pleased to be identified. He seemed as tired as ever, but he pushed himself off the tree trunk and walked along, though his feet dragged.

"Couldn't stop him once he heard," Umber whispered in Lottie's ear. "There's enough of the old Robert left inside that he wanted to come. Took it as a good sign, I did!"

Then the windmill fortress itself came into sight.

It was no less intimidating by the light of day. The mottled gray-and-brown stones took on an even stranger appearance in the sun. They were pitted and rough. As light played across the holes and bumps, each stone shifted in and out of looking like a face. The walls seemed to be built of stacks of lumpy, discolored stone faces, with gaping mouths and hollow eyes.

"Can't say I like the look of that," mumbled Lottie. The wind picked up briefly, and the rusty metal blades of the windmill creaked into action. The groan and cry of the blades was a little less scary to her, now that she could see what it was. If she strained her ears she thought she could hear the voices. Robert visibly tensed up as the sound reached him.

The ground was riddled with tracks, deep muddy ruts crisscrossed in every direction. There were smoldering, smoking pits in the distance, mostly behind the windmill. And a glowing green haze hung overhead. As she looked at the top of the fortress she thought she saw flashes of light sparking out of the highest windows. Umber flinched.

"*Squawk.* You see the signs."

Lottie wondered what was burning in the pits. It was an awful place. *But even worse,* she thought with a shudder, *Lewis might still be inside it.*

Quite a bit of Umber's courage seemed to have left him too as he looked at the signs. He shivered, ducked his head up and down, and ruffled his feathers. He tried to squawk bravely and the sound came out more like a twitter. "There it is," he rattled.

Lottie knelt in the tall grass to catch her breath and make a plan. "Are there any other doors in?" she asked. "Do you know, Robert?"

Robert didn't answer. He wasn't kneeling beside her. She stood up and frantically looked behind them. No Robert.

She turned her head and looked toward the windmill. There, awake and no longer slumbering, walked Robert. He walked tall and straight toward the windmill door. Winding between his feet was the brown cat. Lottie stood up to try to call Robert back, but Umber stopped her. "Mustn't make a noise. We'll be just behind him."

And so it wasn't quite the plan they might have made, but Lottie and Umber marched steadily on toward the fortress, where Robert had already disappeared behind the mottled gray walls.

"Do you think the NightKing is at home?" Lottie asked in a whisper.

"Home? Certainly," Umber creaked.

The NightKing

Lewis stood frozen with fear deep in the windmill fortress, watching his father sleep among the thousands of lengths of cloth. He was thin and pale; his once-brown hair had grown long and stringy and turned mostly gray. His lab coat had many pockets, and draped down past his knees. His long arms and legs looked lost in the folds of gray fabric. His empty eyes gazed blankly into the room.

It was the NightKing's open eyes and vacant stare that made Lewis shiver. This was where his unusual sleep habits had come from. He'd inherited the trait from his father. You'd think his mother might have told him!

And this was why the creatures of LightLand thought the NightKing never slept. He wasn't a threat to them during the day because that's when he was usually sleeping. With his eyes open.

Lewis also felt quite sure that this had to be why he had been left behind in LightLand when Lottie had escaped. He didn't close his eyes, he slept without dreams, and somehow it wasn't enough to separate him from this other world. If he couldn't sleep like everyone else, then he might never get home. Amazingly, the icy sensation thawed and a strange peacefulness settled over Lewis as he understood these things. It wasn't good news, but at least he was beginning to understand.

October looked extremely apprehensive but was steadily creeping forward among the cloths, his nose twitching, as though he were depending on the smell to lead him to the one they needed. Lewis knew from his own experiences that his father was probably a very light sleeper, able to wake up smoothly and know what was going on around him. Lewis moved carefully, trying to *believe* that he would succeed.

It was overwhelming.

As hard as Lewis tried to believe, he was slipping into despair. He silently lifted cloth after cloth, sack after sack, but had no idea how to tell the powerful one from a decoy. He didn't know what he was looking for, or what he would do if he found it. He held a silky-feeling bag up to the light. Something was inside it. . . . Something was moving within it, there were shapes. . . . No, as he reached his hand inside it, he could plainly feel that it was empty. But there were images, pictures, running through the fabric.

Lewis stood transfixed for some time, watching the fluid motion of the pictures that seemed to be woven in the silk, even as they shifted and changed. He saw a young man leaning from the tower of the windmill fortress. The man was waving his arms and calling out, but there was no sound. At first Lewis thought it was himself grown up, a vision from the future. But then, glancing at the NightKing across the room, Lewis wondered if it might more likely be his father, a vision from the past. The young man in the picture looked sad, anxious. What did it mean? Lewis had a hard time putting the sack aside, but he heard the tiny scratching of October's paws and remembered his purpose here.

The next cloth Lewis lifted seemed extraordinarily heavy. It looked like it was made of common burlap, like the farm sacks they used in Iowa to store corn, but when Lewis looked inside, it was full of water. At least it looked like water, only somehow heavier, thicker. It didn't ooze through the roughly woven burlap. It didn't slosh out of the opening when Lewis pulled the sides. He could see his own face reflected in it, and he felt a strong desire to drink. In fact he lowered his face and was about to plunge it below the surface — he could feel his breath bounce off the smooth cold liquid.

Then suddenly something sharp pinched his wrist. Something had bitten him! He stopped and looked up.

October was clinging onto the back of his left hand, having scrambled quickly up Lewis's clothes. It wasn't a real bite, just a nip. But it had been enough. The mouse was shaking his head violently. The pleading look in his tiny black eyes was plain. Lewis, still fighting an intense thirst for the strange water, straightened his back. October thumped his own little chest with his palm, silently begging Lewis to be stronger.

As the two stared intensely at each other, October nodded, trusting him. He let go of Lewis's hand and jumped to the stone floor, rummaging through the piles once more.

Lewis released the water sack. It slogged heavily and silently to the ground, but no liquid ran out. His head ached. *Are you crazy?* Lewis asked himself. *How could you even think about eating or drinking anything in this place?*

Lewis didn't understand yet the power of his father's woven magic. It wasn't due to some weakness that he had almost swallowed that heavy water. There was a strong dark force in the very air of the room. It was weighing down on Lewis, driving him away from all that he knew.

October dropped a cloth and shuddered, moving to the next. He paused and looked at Lewis, checking on him. Lewis nodded gratefully to his friend. He realized that his hands were shaking when he reached into the pile once more.

Suddenly pain shot through the fingers that held the next cloth. The steel gray sack he was holding slipped back to the ground and Lewis gasped. His left hand was really cut. He suppressed his urge to cry out, but a whimper had already escaped him. The sound reverberated in the room, and Lewis turned, panic-stricken, to look at the NightKing.

The steely eyes still blinked and gazed, but the mouth was no longer relaxed. The NightKing turned his face toward Lewis. He saw the bright red cut on Lewis's left hand. His eyes met the frightened eyes of his son.

The NightKing smiled. He smiled an ugly, twisted smile, and Lewis returned the look with a determined glare, ignoring the pain from his hand.

"Wrong choice," his father said, sounding pleased with himself.

Lewis said nothing.

"What are you doing here, Lewis?"

Lewis said nothing.

"Yes, I recognize you. I know who you are. And you know who I am, don't you?"

Lewis said nothing.

"I saw you coming. You and that neighbor girl, Lottie. But why? There's nothing here for you."

Lewis said nothing. He saw the tips of his father's ears turn red. The NightKing was getting angry.

"You still don't speak?" he asked, trying to sound indifferent. "I hadn't realized that. What's wrong with you?"

Lewis said nothing.

"One of these cloths could make you speak to me, you know. It's one of my favorites. I've used it on the rats, giving them speech. Did you notice? It's quite painful, it seems, being forced to speak. The rats scream and flail about. Distressing . . ." The NightKing didn't look distressed. He smiled as he said it, as though remembering something pleasant. "Yes, I'll get it. We'll try that one first. And then perhaps one or two others. Just for fun. So many to choose from, aren't there? Look at them all."

Lewis said nothing. He didn't look around the room. He kept his eyes on his father's face. The NightKing stared back, studying Lewis.

"I can see what the rodents were saying yesterday . . . you do look remarkably like me. Of course I had to punish them for making that mistake. I made three of them come in here. Made them each choose a sack. They picked their own poison, you might say. Oh, they fear this room as much as you do," he chuckled. "I brought them here, to LightLand from my old laboratory in Iowa. I brought dozens of them. They serve me in many ways, but they've been inside my collection here more times than any other creatures. Sometimes they come out again and sometimes they don't."

Lewis said nothing. He clenched his fists. He felt a sticky slippery feeling on his cut left hand. But he still said nothing. His mind began to race. What should he do? He had no plan.

The NightKing was preoccupied. He stared at Lewis but seemed to be seeing something else. "I was your age too when I learned the truth about this strange world. But with a difference. You've discovered that you can get here. I learned that I was *from* here."

Lewis frowned. His father was from LightLand? How was that possible? He wanted to ask, but still he said nothing. Without realizing he was doing it, Lewis shook his head. His father scoffed.

"Have they told you that I have no beginning and no end? It's true, actually. Neither do they, though they don't realize it. No one in LightLand is born and no one dies. They simply do — or do not — exist in a vague state of being remembered and forgotten. LightLand. Ha!"

The look on his father's face was puzzling. Why was he being told all this? Although Lewis had no plan, he worried that the NightKing did. His eyes jerked left and right as he checked the stone chamber for a way to distract the NightKing, a way to get past him to the heavy door on the other side of the room.

The NightKing's piercing eyes saw through his thoughts.

"You can't escape. I'm just trying to decide what to do with you, Lewis. I wonder, is there any reason to keep you around?"

This time Lewis actually opened his mouth to respond. The words froze on his tongue and he hesitated. Did he need more time to think? Was he ready to speak? He closed his mouth and swallowed hard.

The NightKing muttered with disgust and turned his back, staring toward the door.

Lewis almost smiled. He was amazed at himself. His own father stood there threatening to kill him, and he wasn't afraid. He had withdrawn from the world his entire life by refusing to speak, but with a surge of adrenaline rushing through him, he realized that it didn't matter to him anymore. He didn't need to hide. He was ready.

This is the time, Lewis thought. He'd been silent long enough. And then Lewis spoke.

"I remember you," he said simply.

The dark hunched back didn't turn, but Lewis felt that he was listening.

"P-people here say you don't have a story of your own, but that's wrong. You do. I-I-I remember it. You say you're from here, but that's wrong, too. That isn't your story. You aren't from LightLand at all.

"Y-you were born in Topeka, Kansas, on-on-on a hot summer day. When you were my size, you caught crayfish for your grandfather and he paid you a nickel apiece. You told me that story. And I remember it," Lewis said.

"You were the tallest boy in the twelfth grade and you met a girl named Lucille, and she is my mother. She misses you and she hates you, and . . . and so do I." By the time he finished, Lewis felt as though he couldn't breathe.

The NightKing slowly turned. Lewis had tried to reach something decent and human deep inside of him, had tried to make him *feel* something, remember something *real*. Looking into his father's eyes, Lewis couldn't tell. They stared past him. Was he remembering?

"Yes," the NightKing answered, as though Lewis had spoken this last thought aloud. "Of course I remember."

Lewis held his breath. It couldn't be as easy as that.

"It's a myth that was concocted by the creatures here in LightLand — the idea that I have no memory of my own. Of course I do. My memory is, in fact, perfect." The NightKing sighed and looked, somehow, tired.

"It's what drew me to this science. My studies interested me because I grew so frustrated with the feeble memories of others. I'm discovering many ways to concentrate memory, intensify it. I can use it to serve my own purposes. Others' inability to preserve the past within their minds still disgusts me. My science seeks to remedy this weakness."

"Science?" Lewis croaked, scoffing quietly. "You call what you're doing science?"

The NightKing ignored the question. "I've thought of you, Lewis. Not often, but sometimes I've wondered . . . about your pathetic, silent little life in Iowa. You and your mother."

Lewis wasn't certain, but he thought there was a gasp of sadness in the voice, though the eyes remained vague and empty.

"Sh-she's lonely," Lewis prodded. "Nothing pleases her. Ever. I don't think she was always like that. . . ."

"Actually, you're wrong," his father answered in a matter-of-fact voice. "She *was*. I think it's what attracted me. She puzzled me. Unwilling to be happy. I understand it better now. What use is happiness? Lucille had no desire for it. Now I have no time for it."

Lucille. He sounded almost human when he said her name. Lewis felt a flutter of hope in his throat. Maybe it would be this easy. "Th-that could change," he said.

But then the eyes Lewis saw glaring down at him flashed in anger. In his bony, pale hands, the NightKing held one of the cloths. It was thick, black, and smudged, dirty. Soft gray ropes dangled from it. Lewis swallowed with difficulty, wondering if he'd be able to breathe from inside the sack.

The NightKing hissed, "That was enough . . . I've heard all I care to from you, Lewis. Glad to know that you *can* speak. Not some genetic weakness that I have to be concerned with, just your own insipid eccentricity. But I'll have nothing more to do with you now. I don't think I want your wheedling voice echoing through my halls. Did you and your little friend think I accepted any and all voices for my studies? My science will progress faster when you are no longer a distraction."

Lewis's mouth hung open in surprise. He'd thought that he'd broken through. It was so hard to think. . . . His left hand stung where it had been cut. His head ached. He grasped for something to distract the NightKing. "Science — I'm good at science, you know," he stuttered. "N-nobody says it, but I know they think it, that I'm like you. That I might be a-a-a scientist someday. Like you." He felt sick at his own words and hoped desperately that it wasn't true, that he wasn't — couldn't be — anything like his father.

Lewis tried not to choke as he said it again. "I might be like you."

"Ah, Lewis." The voice was mild and indifferent. "There are many things you might have been."

The NightKing stretched the ropes and snapped them between his hands. He took a step closer to Lewis. Lewis stood his ground, his eyes nervously bouncing between the ropes and his father's cold eyes.

"Wh-what about the other sacks?"

"What?" the NightKing asked, irritated. "What about them?"

"They're all dangerous? Sh-show them to me. . . ."

"Yes. I've woven each of them with dangerous memories, distilled, intensified." The NightKing gave a little laugh. "It's been like a hobby for me, you could say. Some are poisonous to the touch. Others burst into flames if moved. Several may appear soft but — as you've seen — can shred your fingers. It interests you, does it?"

"But there are so many. How — how do you know which is which?" Lewis asked in a small voice, just determined to continue speaking.

"I alone know the difference," he growled.

"But . . . why?" Lewis was beginning to feel light-headed.

"Power," the NightKing rumbled. "Memories that intensify instead of fading . . . Are you too stupid to see the power? Here in this weak world, where memory is all-important, I am all-powerful! If I control memory, I control LightLand. And forever!" he thundered. The NightKing had lost his patience.

"Is that," Lewis whispered, "the Veil of Oblivion?"

"You expect me to teach you my secrets?! You want to know if this, this rag is the first one I wove? The Veil of Oblivion?"

"Is it?" Lewis asked quietly, trying to keep his voice steady, though his hands trembled at his sides.

Lewis gasped as the NightKing wrapped the ropes around his hands but let the cloth slip to the floor. "No, Lewis, it's not."

For a brief instant, Lewis felt relieved, but when the icy look in his father's eyes only sharpened, Lewis took a step backward.

"I've used that cloth," he said, stepping on the thick, black sack at his feet, "once or twice. Inside that one you would hear endless shrieking. It was woven while we tortured a few useless citizens of LightLand. The fabric remembers, you see. It preserves their screams for all time, and it magnifies them as well. The decibels are so piercing that your eardrums would split in two and you would never hear anything again. Want to try it, Lewis?"

Lewis shook his head.

"I put an irritating rat into it last year. In minutes the rat lost both its hearing and its mind — useless now. But standing out here, outside the cloth, I heard nothing at all! Not the screams that are woven inside, not the screams of the stupid rat, nothing. Each thing I weave is precious. But only one is the Veil of Oblivion. It is the heart of my science of memory."

"This is *not* science," Lewis muttered, unable to censor his words. "Your miserable torture collection? You're supposed to be brilliant and this is the best you can do?"

The NightKing turned purple with rage. "THAT'S ENOUGH! QUIET!"

"I won't. I'm — I'm not afraid of you." Lewis watched his father's face carefully. It twisted and he looked like he was in pain.

"You should be, Lewis. You should be afraid."

Lewis put up his hands as though to stop the NightKing's advance. The sight of Lewis's injured left hand made his father pause. He stared. His eyes glazed over for a minute. He opened his mouth to speak but hesitated. A single drop of blood from Lewis's hand splashed on the stone floor between them.

Time seemed to stand still as they both stared at the speck of red on the cold gray stone. Then their eyes connected once more.

"Wait —" the NightKing said with a mean smile. "You interest me, Lewis. I'm not quite sure why. But you think that you are as smart as I am, do you? Why don't we give you a chance to prove it?

"Let's see if you can do better with my collection. Yes. I'll give you another chance. I'll give you . . . an hour. Let's see if you can find the first cloth, the Veil of Oblivion, or if you finish yourself off in the process." The NightKing laughed quietly as Lewis's eyes flickered over the thousands of cloths in the room.

"Some of them are decoys, of course. Many are truly deadly. I'll be interested to see what happens to you. Find the Veil and perhaps I'll let you join me. Give you the job of a rat!" He turned to go but then paused. He looked back with a very strange expression.

"Oh, yes, and Lewis?"

Lewis swallowed and returned the stare.

"One of the sacks will bring you freedom." The NightKing laughed again. "That's right. It's woven with all the memories of *home*," he sneered. "It would take you back to your precious Iowa. Good luck, then. I'll return to see how you've made out. I expect you'll have done the dirty work for me."

And with one last strange piercing look, the NightKing was gone, and Lewis heard the door being barred from the outside.

CHAPTER TEN

The Room Below the Mill

Just inside the entrance to the windmill, Lottie and Umber could hear the mixed-up mumbling, moaning of the voices in the NightKing's collection. Next they heard the scratching, clattering sounds of the laboratory animals. Lottie shivered with goose bumps. *How could Lewis still be in here?* Suddenly something stepped out of the shadows.

Lottie choked back a scream. Was it the NightKing?

The tall yellow-haired young man in front of her looked so familiar.

"*Squawk?* Robert?" Umber whistled hoarsely.

Robert was transformed. His blue eyes were deep and clear. Light seemed to shine from his pupils. His gaze was steady and strong. He was taller. He nodded. He had his spirit back. There could be no doubt.

"I'll follow you now, Lottie Cook," he said.

"But how — what did you —" Lottie spluttered quietly. "What *happened*?"

Umber clucked and shook his head at her. "Not now," he squawked in a whisper to Lottie. "We are following you."

Lottie walked on, but she was distracted by Robert's appearance. Suddenly she looked around her and realized that they should have come to the stairs by now. Where were they? Had she missed a turn? Umber settled himself on Robert's shoulder and was watching Lottie intently. She was leading them, but she didn't know where she was.

The green glow from the walls disoriented her. Lottie swallowed hard and indicated with a jerk of her head that they should keep walking forward. Looking straight ahead was as good as anywhere else.

The corridor turned in circles upon itself, and it dawned on Lottie that it was sloping slightly upward. She saw dark cracks in the walls near the ceiling and floor, but she didn't realize that they were being watched.

Suddenly three giant rats stepped out in front of them, baring their sharp teeth and holding their ropey tails like whips. Lottie groped wildly in her clothes for something to use as a weapon against these monsters. Of course, she was wearing only her pajamas. All she had in her pocket was Lewis's little notebook. She held the tiny cherry seed in the hem of her shirt as though it were a good luck charm. She gritted her teeth.

She shot a glance at Robert, who had assumed the stance of a boxer with his fists in the air. The cat at his feet hissed. Robert scuffed his shoes on the stone floor. Lottie wore only her soft-soled slippers. Kicking wouldn't even be effective. They were unarmed. . . . How had they thought they were going to defend themselves? They should have carried sticks, torches, stones, anything.

Then the smallest rat spoke.

"The famous Lottie Cook, isn't it?" The other rats laughed in an ugly sneering way. "You're the one he wants, right?" The others bobbed their pointy heads and made horrible sucking noises through their teeth.

"Who wants to see me?" Lottie asked loudly, and the rats were startled by the echoing boom of her voice.

The biggest rat, the one in the center, twitched his whiskers. "He is the NightKing, Lottie Cook. And he'll do more than see you." The rat leered in closer to her, hissing as it spoke. "He'll destroy you."

"Then he'll have to destroy me as well," Robert grunted, stepping closer to the rats. The two smaller ones slid slightly behind their leader.

Suddenly Umber burst from Robert's shoulder with a crazy howl, flying straight at the center rat. The flash of color terrified and paralyzed the rats, but it mobilized Robert and Lottie. In a wild moment of noise and motion, they dove at the rats.

Umber was in the biggest one's face, squawking ferociously. The bird managed to dodge the rat's flailing claws. Robert's cat joined Umber and chased from the other side. Robert lunged forward and managed to grasp the ropey tail of the rat on the left and used it to pull the creature off its scratchy feet.

Lottie faced the rat on the right. It was smaller but quicker than the other two. Before she knew what was happening, Lottie felt her hands being bound by sharp twists of the rat's tail. She resisted wildly, but the rat grabbed her by the hair and dragged her from the room.

Her screams were lost in the echoing chaos. Robert and Umber looked up only in time to see her disappear into a dark crack in the stone. When they had disentangled themselves and reached the wall, the crack had closed and Lottie was gone.

Robert pounded furiously on the stone. The rat that he had thrown headlong into the opposite wall lay crumpled on the floor, but it managed to lift its head and laugh at them.

"Where did he take her, rat?" Robert demanded.

"Bah," the rat spat at them.

Robert glowered at the disgusting creature. "Where is she?!"

Umber's rat was curled in a ball in the corner. "You've lost that one," it sneered, wheezing for breath. "And you're trapped as well. . . ."

Robert lifted the crumpled rat by the scruff of its neck. "Open the wall," he growled. "Do it now."

"Bah," the rat spit again. "Or what will you do to me? Kill me? Go ahead. I'd as soon be killed by you as stuffed into one of his sacks. . . ."

"Ha!" The other rat joined in. "That's waiting for us now, the Veil for sure. Nothing worse you can do."

Robert shoved the rat into the wall where Lottie had disappeared. "Open it. Do it now."

"Bah, bah!" the rats croaked. "Do it yourself. Do it yourself if you dare."

Umber fluttered clumsily to Robert's shoulder. "We can do it. It has to be simple. If they can do it, we can do it. *Squawk.*" The bird looked with contempt at the rats on the floor.

Robert pressed his hands on the wall. Nothing happened. "She's in there, somehow," Robert fumed. He tried again, this time just barely grazing the stone with his fingertips. His head was pounding, but his hands hovered there, barely touching the wall. *It has to open,* he thought. *It will open because it has to open.* And that was all it took.

The crack slid silently open. Easily wide and tall enough for Robert and Umber to pass through, leaving the disappointed and injured rats behind them.

*   *   *

Lottie was long gone by the time her friends passed through. She had been dragged down between the walls of the old windmill. Cracks shifted and opened and closed again at the slightest touch from the rat. Lottie frantically tried to memorize the direction, but it was futile. How could she open and close these solid rock walls? It was magic, and she didn't understand it. And even if she could figure out how to do it, she'd never be able to retrace their steps.

The rat was huffing and puffing as he hauled Lottie to their final destination. There were small, high windows ahead of them, and Lottie could see grass growing around the window well. It was a room just below ground level, like a basement. The windows looked out behind the mill. Lottie could see the smokey fire pits that she'd glimpsed on her way inside. She grimly estimated that the windows were ten or twelve feet from the floor. It would be difficult to reach them, but they seemed to be her best chance of escape. At least she'd be able to find her way if she could get outside.

The ceiling of the room was a tangled mess of gears and electrical wiring. There was a large generator, evidently powered by the eight long arms that turned in the wind high above them. This motor was built into a kind of loft at ceiling level. Thick, insulated wires snaked down the walls and across the floor to oversize looms that filled the space.

It had been outfitted as a textile mill. The electricity that was captured from the wind was channeled here, below ground, to these machines that could be used to weave fabric. The rat dropped Lottie and looked around nervously. There was no one else in the room, but the rat was clearly expecting someone.

"Should tie you up," it grunted with great annoyance.

There was plenty of rope. The room had barrels of rope and chain and cording and straps and ribbon and strips of strange fabric remnants. But the rat looked around despairingly, as though there were nothing to use. He didn't even seem to consider touching any of these things.

Lottie didn't understand this hesitation, but she certainly wasn't about to make any suggestions. She rubbed her sore limbs and gingerly touched her face. Her cheek was scratched raw.

The rat made a high screeching sound. Lottie could just barely hear it, the pitch was so high. In answer to the call, Lottie heard scratchy scampering footsteps. Two white lab mice appeared in the doorway. They were smaller than the rat but enormous for mice.

The rat gestured toward Lottie. "Know who that is?" he asked with a snarl. The mice nodded nervously. "Well, keep her in here. I'm going to make the report, understand?"

The mice nodded again, terrified this time. They clearly

didn't appear to be up to the job of guarding her, Lottie thought. She felt certain she could knock them both over with one good push and make her way out of the door. The question was, what would she do after that? Which way would she go? She didn't know.

The big rat stormed out impatiently with one last glare at Lottie, half of its ugly mouth curved in a grotesque smile. It seemed very pleased to be placing responsibility on these underlings and getting out of the room. As his scratchy, self-important footsteps echoed through the stone chamber, the two young guard mice stared at her apprehensively.

"L-L-Lottie Cook?" one of them whispered. Lottie nodded.

"How do you know who I am?" she asked quietly, trying not to frighten the skittish mice. *They* would know the way out. She hoped she might trick them into helping her.

The same mouse gasped a little. "We hear! His Kingship curses your name. The stones repeat it!" The other mouse gave him a threatening look, clearly wanting him to shut up.

"But why?" Lottie asked. She didn't so much expect the mice to tell her. She was really just thinking out loud.

"Your memory is strong, Lottie Cook. He knows it. The tree grew. Nothing new should grow in his lands any-more. He keeps tight control. But he saw the tree you grew. He fears it."

The silent mouse was shaking now. It looked as though it

might run away any minute. Lottie reached down to the hem of her pajamas and felt the cherry pit. "He's afraid of my cherry tree?" she asked.

Finally the second mouse spoke. "Not afraid of anything! Angry!" The mouse stamped its foot and glared. The first mouse clapped its paws over its mouth.

Lottie wasn't sure if she'd get much more information from these frightened guards. But she was fairly certain that she didn't have to worry about them. They wouldn't hurt her. She could storm past them if she tried. But first, she ought to have some sort of plan.

She got to her feet and walked around the room. The mice were quite clearly uncomfortable with this, but they didn't say anything to her. They just kept looking nervously at each other.

Lottie walked to the looms and looked at the pinkish fabric being stretched across them. It was glowing softly. Lottie longed to feel it. When she reached out her hand to touch it, the first mouse cried out, as if to stop her. Lottie gave the mouse a puzzled look.

"Why shouldn't I touch it?" she asked. The second mouse glared at the first and neither one answered.

Lottie reached out her hand again. The first mouse's whimpering gave her a moment's pause, but she couldn't stop herself. She went ahead and touched the cloth.

*　*　*

It is hard to describe what happened next.

Time and space exploded. Or imploded. With Lottie Cook at the center. It was deepest night, brightest day. She was flying; she was diving. Silence, chaos. Again and again, blinding light echoed against vibrating darkness. Time expanded and contracted. The next moment that she was fully conscious, Lottie trembled like a leaf in a storm. Her eyes were closed, and she was afraid to move.

She had remembered. . . . No, it was more than that. Beyond mere memory. It had been real. . . . The sound of a voice humming, waiting for tea water to boil. . . .

She had been with her mother again.

Lottie didn't want to open her eyes. Afraid of what she would see, or wouldn't see, she tried to stop her hands from shaking so. She didn't breathe for several minutes then suddenly, without realizing it, gasped ferociously, sucking in the air with painful gulps.

It had been on her mind, on the very back edge of her mind, ever since Zerox had appeared that night with Lewis. If he had remembered the dogs and they had come, what else was possible? If she could create an image of her grandfather, why not others? She had pushed the thought of her mother back, back into the impossible. She had been afraid to even contemplate it. But now she was sure it had happened.

Lottie had remembered her. And she had come.

She couldn't find the details in her stunned mind. For the moment she couldn't even remember what her mother looked like in the treasured photographs that Lottie kept in her top dresser drawer at home. But she could feel it. She could feel her mother's presence.

The Cloth, Lottie thought, mouth still gaping, eyes still closed. Her fingers were empty, she must have dropped it. She was afraid to touch it again, and yet . . . and yet she longed to touch it again. Cautiously, she opened her eyes.

The room was unrecognizable. It looked as though it had melted. The very stone was blasted smooth and glistening, glowing almost white. The door and windows had vanished into a molten wall of transformed stone. She was alone.

There was absolutely no sign of the two young mice who had stood guard. No trace of the looms and spinning wheels. Not a thread remained of the baskets of cloth, strings, ropes, chains, yarn.

There was nothing. Especially not her mother.

There was only Lottie.

CHAPTER ELEVEN

The Veil of Oblivion

High above in the windmill fortress of the NightKing, Lewis felt the floor he was standing on tremble. He didn't know what magic might be surging through the building. Lewis had no idea that it was Lottie, deep below, who had rocked and melted the massive stone walls.

Now that the NightKing had left, locking Lewis in the room with his collection, he felt every muscle in his body quiver and collapse. He slumped to his knees and looked around, bewildered. How had he survived that confrontation with his father? October emerged from his hiding place and Lewis felt the slightest, gentlest touch from one tiny paw on his left hand.

Lewis took a deep breath. He felt both a shivering relief and overwhelming dread. His injured hand tingled and

175

burned. He had to wrap it up. Looking at the vast pile of cloths, Lewis decided to choose one. He would tear one and use a strip as a bandage.

Most of the sacks weren't fit to use. They were either too rough or too heavy to tear, too dirty or too sharp to put on his skin. Lewis moved into the middle of the room and searched with his eyes. He saw a bit of something that looked like soft flannel.

It was incredibly soft. Lewis pulled the pale yellow bag out of the pile. It was clean and thin, the size of a pillow case. October gasped as, without even hesitating, Lewis held the bag up firmly with his right hand, grabbed the top between his teeth, and yanked with all of his might.

The soft fabric tore neatly. Lewis ripped it lengthwise into a long bandage, threw the remainder back on the pile, and began to wrap his hand. October scurried over with a look of pure amazement on his face. He helped Lewis pull the fabric tight and tied a knot over the back of his hand.

Lewis expected the blood to soak through the pale yellow bandage easily, but it didn't. Within minutes, he felt much, much better. The color returned to his cheeks. He wiggled his fingers and was surprised that they felt all right. Better than that, they felt . . . strong. Not sure why, Lewis retrieved the rest of the torn yellow bag and stuffed the soft cloth into his back pocket.

"You — you spoke," October whispered.

Lewis nodded and then said, "Yes."

And then he actually laughed. The mouse was so startled that he tumbled over. Real laughter had perhaps never been heard in this cold room. Lewis's small laugh bounced back and forth off the walls. And then something strange happened.

The pile of sacks shifted. Lewis and October both gasped. Had they imagined it? Suddenly the pile seemed smaller than it had just seconds before.

"We have an hour, then," Lewis said, his eyes wide, studying the pile.

October nodded. They began moving the bags and sacks and sheets. They worked by instinct, not knowing if they were making the right choices. They started forming a rejects pile of sacks they believed to be useless. Bags that just seemed *wrong* somehow. First in the rejects pile were all the sheets made of metal. They clinked and landed heavily in the corner.

For some reason, Lewis found himself moving the sacks with his left hand, the one wrapped in the yellow bandage. His fingers no longer hurt, and it somehow seemed safer to him.

October scurried among the bags, sniffing, prodding. One sack, woven of a strange papery crepe, burst into flames when the mouse poked his head inside. The poor mouse barely escaped. Lewis came trampling over and put out the fire by stamping on it with his boots.

Still, even when his boots smoked and smelled of singed leather, even when he saw the fear in his small friend's eyes, Lewis was lighthearted.

He knew that he stood a chance. Maybe it wasn't quite likely that he would escape in one piece, but he didn't face certain doom. And it cheered him to think about how he had stood up to his father.

Then he reached for a shimmery, floaty-looking bag, but before he could put his fingers on it, it was gone. Lewis gasped and October ran over, expecting another fire or worse.

When Lewis tried to describe it to Lottie later, he said that it seemed like some of the sacks were *mirages.* They were decoys, images that vanished before he could touch them.

Time slipped away as they sifted through the room. Lewis couldn't be sure, but he thought that more than an hour had passed. Much more than an hour. Why hadn't his father returned?

The NightKing had not returned because he was busy. Things were unraveling.

The explosion in the room below the mill had been felt throughout the fortress. The walls shook, the floors trembled, stones melted and fused, and many passageways that had appeared to be solid rock seemed to vanish. As Lottie and Lewis understood it later, much of the fortress was created from magic, just like the mirage sacks that Lewis had discovered. When the explosion rocked the foundation of the windmill, these illusions disappeared.

Robert and Umber suddenly found themselves racing through wide clean halls as they searched for Lottie. There was no need to weave through narrow, dark gaps in the rock. They whooped with excitement as they ran. Somehow this had to be good, they thought. Things were changing.

Indeed, in the very top tower room, where Lewis had stomped on the rat's tail days before, the NightKing himself felt the blast. The rodents at his feet squealed in fear and huddled in a terrified heap. They burrowed and fought to be at the bottom of the pile. The fortress shook; what did it mean?

The NightKing kicked the mass of rats and lab mice, and many of them flew across the room, smashing into the wall. Then they did something that they would not have dared to do just a day before: They ran for their lives. They disappeared into holes and tunnels.

"Fools!" the NightKing roared. "It's nothing! You'll pay a price for being cowards!" But it was too late. All but the largest rats had gone into hiding. The few that were still there clawed at one another, trying to hide at the bottom of the small squirming pile that remained.

The NightKing knew what had happened. He kicked the

frightened heap of rats once more and stormed down the stairs. He had to stop Lottie Cook. If he wasn't too late already.

Lewis was not giving up. October scurried tirelessly about the room, dragging some bags into the slowly growing pile by the door. Lewis's shirtsleeves caught fire when one sack exploded as he raised it up. He put the fire out quickly enough and wasn't hurt. Another one seemed to turn to glass, and diamondlike splinters covered him, scratching his face and hands even as he tried to brush them off.

And then something caught his eye.

It had been way off to the side. He couldn't believe that he hadn't seen it before. It was such a strange, deep color. Scarlet, but almost molten. The color seemed to throb and change as he looked at it. He was afraid at first to touch it. Would it be hot? It looked like fire itself.

He had to touch it.

It was cold. It was icy and seemed to freeze his insides as he put his fingers on it. Lewis was afraid, but he wasn't letting go. And then the sensation changed. The icy coldness washed away. The scarlet color was still deep, burning red, but sheer; he could see his hand through it. Lewis could feel energy surging through the threads. This cloth was powerful, more so than any of the others he had sorted. It was in a different league. But was it the Veil of Oblivion?

Suddenly Lewis heard a muffled, heavy, clanking sound from the other side of the door.

Terrified, he turned his head. Someone was unlocking the bolt. Lewis braced himself to face his father again. He was prepared to fight. The cloth he held tingled. . . . It meant something. He held the cloth up like a weapon, ready to challenge the NightKing.

But it wasn't the NightKing. Lewis stared in amazement when the door creaked open. A tall yellow-haired young man was in the entryway. A gust of air blew in with him. His face was stiff with determination and his eyes flashed. There was a brown cat threading through his feet.

Of course, it was Robert.

October's head was bobbing up and down with happiness.

Robert's eyes took in the thousand sacks spread about the room. He saw the sheer, scarlet cloth Lewis was holding up to the light. A chill of recognition slipped across his face. He remembered it and nodded. That was it: the Veil of Oblivion. Robert's strong, tired face was certain.

There was a frantic flapping sound from the stone corridor. Lewis gripped the Veil more tightly and Robert turned.

"*Squawk —*" Umber creaked quietly as he flew around the doorway. Lewis thought that this had to be Lottie's bird. Umber landed on Robert's shoulder and stared. Lewis regarded the two strangers. He didn't know them, and yet he trusted them somehow. If *they* were here, Lewis thought, then Lottie couldn't be far.

Umber shuddered as he studied the NightKing's son. The resemblance was powerful — but incomplete. Umber had to admit that the warmth in Lewis's brown eyes was clear and deep. This warmth made all the difference in the world.

Introductions would wait. With his left hand, Lewis held the scarlet Veil up high for them all to see. They understood one another. They had accomplished the mission; they had seized the Veil. Now they needed to escape with it. But there was one question that tumbled out of each mouth . . .

"Where is Lottie?" three hushed voices asked simultaneously. None of them knew the answer.

"She's here. But she's been captured," Robert whispered, and Lewis's heart sank. Now he couldn't escape. He had to find Lottie first.

Desperation flickered across their eyes as the fortress suddenly shook with yet another explosion. Lewis felt a small scratching on his boot and bent down to scoop up the mouse in his right hand, bringing him to eye level.

"*Squawk!* October Mouse! Where did you come from? Where have you been?"

"Quiet, Umber," October chided, but with a pleased smile. "We must remove the Veil, but the passages are no longer safe. We will leave by the windows at once."

"By the windows!" Lewis was incredulous. "We've got to be six stories up."

"We'll use these," the mouse insisted. It scampered down the side of Lewis and ran to a small pile of sacks that it had stowed near the door. "These are harmless. Decoys. Enough for each of us, I think."

Robert gathered the sacks and carried them into the hall, following October, though he didn't fully realize what the mouse was planning. Lewis thought he understood. Several of the sacks, as he had sorted them, had reminded him of thin, filmy parachute cloth. The mouse meant for them to jump!

The corridor outside the central room was lined with deep-set windows. Leaning over the stone sill and looking out, Lewis felt his head reeling dizzily. They were much too high up. He'd never be able to do this.

"W-what about Lottie? I can't leave her here." Lewis's pulse raced as he thought about confronting his father again.

"We won't leave without her. We'll split up," Robert offered. "Umber, you take the Veil of Oblivion. You can carry it and fly far to a safe place."

Umber looked terrified and backed away as Lewis moved to give him the fiery fabric. "It's all right," Lewis said, trying to reassure him. "It's all right to touch it. I've been touching it, and I'm all right."

They looked Lewis over, his bandaged hand, his dirty

scratched-up face, his torn clothes and singed shirtsleeves, his flame-blackened boots. "I mean. I'm all right *really*," he insisted.

The bird anxiously stretched out his three-toed foot to take the Veil. Lewis tried to give it to him. Meant to give it to him.

Something was wrong.

Lewis wanted to give the Veil to Umber. Knew he should give it to the bird. But instead he stepped backward. The magic of the NightKing was affecting him. His fingers turned white as he clasped the cloth. He should have been releasing it, but his grip just closed harder. The color drained from his face as he struggled. He bit his lip until it hurt and took another step in the wrong direction.

The others looked at Lewis with shock. Umber thought he knew just what this meant. Perhaps Lewis and the NightKing *were* one. Perhaps he, Umber, had been right all along not to trust Lewis.

Beneath their feet the fortress shuddered with a third explosion.

Lewis was panicked. He wanted to hand over the cloth, but he couldn't move his arm. Once again, his small new friend came to his rescue. October the True Mouse raced up Lewis's sleeve and whispered urgently in his ear, tugging and scratching, trying to break the hold of the NightKing's magic.

Whatever October said to him, Lewis never remembered.

He fell to his knees and, with the mouse's help, pried open his fingers and released the Veil.

As soon as the Veil was out of his hands, he felt as though he'd returned to himself. His fingers were stiff and cold from clutching the strange fabric, but his mind was once again his own.

Umber nodded, just once, and took it. Bravely, the bird clutched the scarlet Veil and trembled as the tingling feeling ruffled his feathers. Then without looking back, he hurtled from the window. They all leaned over to watch. Lewis thought he was going to be sick as he saw the blur of lopsided color speeding to the ground. But Umber gained control in time and, without landing, began bumbling away, as far from the fortress and as quickly as he could manage. The Veil of Oblivion shimmered behind him and almost made it look as though the bird was on fire.

Now October wanted Robert to jump, to go and rally as many citizens of LightLand as he could find, bringing them out of hiding. Robert wanted to stay and find Lottie. Her coming to LightLand had saved him, and he wanted to help her now.

"*You* should jump," Robert told Lewis, holding a parachute sack out to him. "You need to escape; you've been through enough. Lottie may be out of the fortress already anyway. I will stay and search for her in case she's still inside."

The building shook again. Lewis desperately wanted to escape from the NightKing's windmill. But jump from the window? He couldn't possibly. He *couldn't* jump from that window. Robert put his hand on his shoulder. "Are you all right?"

Lewis made this choice: He let his fear make him brave. He nodded. He might have to face his father again, but he needed to find Lottie. "I want to stay," he said. "I have to stay." Once he spoke the words, they were true. Nothing could have changed his mind.

So, shaking his head regretfully, Robert climbed back up in the wide stone windowsill, grasped three cloth sacks in his fists, and jumped.

Lewis couldn't watch.

It wasn't until October cheered that Lewis could even look up. Then he leaned anxiously from the windowsill. Way down below he could see the stark yellow head of Robert. Finally he managed to wave.

Lewis felt the outside air on his scratched face, and for just a moment he saw himself. He could envision how he must look in the chilly daylight. His face was transformed by grime and fatigue. He leaned from the high fortress, waving, and realized it was the image he had seen played in the magic cloth of the bag in the room behind him. It had been an image of himself after all. Not older, but changed.

He leaned even farther and called to Robert, "Watch for

Lottie!" Robert waved in return and then, leaving the three parachute sacks behind on the ground, began to run after Umber. Lewis pulled his head back inside.

October climbed quickly to Lewis's shoulder. "I will ride," he said. "Let us search."

The massive stones rattled again below them as they began their quest for Lottie. Robert's cat followed Lewis now. The twisting halls were like a maze. As the passages crumbled, the voices that had been captured by the Veil echoed wildly and vanished. Lewis moved quickly, looking into every room they passed. Sometimes a room seemed so familiar, he thought he must have already checked it.

What Lewis didn't understand was the complex construction of the windmill. There were still dozens of secret passages that remained and turned around on themselves. They had been built into the thick stone walls when the fortress was first erected. The NightKing preferred moving invisibly within these walls.

At the base of the mill Lottie still stood shuddering in the blasted remains of the weaving room. Even though this room had been all but obliterated when she touched the cloth on the loom, the NightKing could appear as if from nowhere.

And he did.

Lottie screamed. The NightKing smiled. This pleased him.

"Lottie Cook," he mocked. "What have you done to my room?"

"You . . ." she gasped. "It's you. . . ."

Of course, Lottie recognized him. It sent her head spinning. Umber had been right in a way. Lewis and the NightKing — not one and the same — but father and son. She tried to steady herself.

"It's too bad you didn't touch the loom with both hands," he said. "The blast of memory then might have killed you."

"I was with my mother," Lottie said without meaning to speak at all.

"How sweet," the NightKing purred. "But you didn't dare to try and force her memory on your own, did you? You could have done it all along, you know. You evoked your grandfather," he sneered. "But you didn't dare call on your strongest memories. Too cowardly to re-create your own mother."

"I could have?" Lottie gasped. "All along?"

"Of course. There is no limit, really, to the force of memory here. In this room, I have woven that force into cloth. Some show the past. Some, I believe, show the future. Memory of the past predicts the future with remarkable accuracy, and history, as it is said, is destiny. I've seen you in many of these cloths, Lottie. For some reason, I am linked to you."

Lottie shuddered.

"I've struggled to understand it." The NightKing nodded. "Somehow you and Lewis persist in my own future. When I study the veils to try and see what happens to *me,* I see only *you.* Or sometimes the two of you. I will not be carried into the future by the memories of two children."

Lottie stared at him. *She* carried the future memories of the NightKing?

"Your insipid stories buzz through my world here. Your cherry trees and cornfields." He almost seemed to growl at the thought. "Yes, your memories are powerful, and it's a power that is not under my control. Yet.

"I plan to put a stop to it. Today. By controlling memory, I control my destiny. I'll start by wiping out *your* memory. . . . It's interfering with my own." He smiled in a way that chilled Lottie's blood. She fumbled in her pajama shirt and tried to get a hold of the cherry seed tied there. Her hands were numb and clumsy.

"Let me help you meet that mother of yours again," the NightKing smiled coldly. Lottie couldn't find the seed. She groped more frantically. She had it but couldn't untie it. The NightKing was reaching toward her. Her fingers were too stiff.

"Our dear Lewis can help, too," the NightKing purred. "If he isn't dead already." And with that he put an icy hand on Lottie's neck.

Everything went dark.

Lottie swam in her own thoughts. She couldn't pull out of the blackness, she couldn't feel her own body, didn't know what was happening to her.

The NightKing had poisoned her slightly with the cold touch of his hand. She fell, unconscious, to the floor. Then he began dragging her through the secret tunnels up to the highest room, where he had left Lewis locked behind the door.

It was his own greed that turned the tide at that moment. He wanted to trap the power of Lottie's memory within his collection, but Lottie had demolished his weaving room. Now he would have to spill her mind into the Veil of Oblivion.

Of course, while the NightKing moved with great speed *within* the walls, Lewis and October raced through the twisting hallways in the other direction. They passed each other without knowing it because a thick wall of stone separated them.

When the NightKing reached the innermost room and found it open and empty, he stomped in with a fit of anger. Lewis heard the sound echoing through the windmill and he spun about and followed. He ran as fast as he could.

The NightKing dropped Lottie hard on the floor and surveyed the room. The piles of sorted sacks infuriated him. He had expected to find his worthless son sprawled lifeless, and instead, his deadly collection had been rifled through, played with! Where was it? Where was his Veil? He needed it for Lottie Cook.

Lewis somehow sensed what was happening. He ran full out. He had to get back to the top of the tower.

The NightKing was in a rage. Lottie had hit the floor hard enough to jar her back to consciousness. She felt herself swimming out of darkness and opened her eyes. She could hear the NightKing cursing and stomping around the room, throwing sacks left and right. Just inches from Lottie's face she noticed something. It looked like corn husks.

Lottie heard the thumping sounds of Lewis's feet as he came closer, but she thought it was the pounding of her own heart. Groggy, she tried to understand what she saw. Corn husks? No, it was something else.

Lewis neared the room and tried to restrain himself from calling out, but he couldn't stop. "LOTTIE!"

The NightKing heard his son's voice and reached for a blue sack. It didn't have the mysterious soul-stealing powers of the Veil of Oblivion. It was deadly. Without exception. He had been foolish for delaying the inevitable, he thought with disgust. This was all his own fault — he should have finished Lewis off the first time he saw him.

"LOTTIE!" Lewis was almost to the room.

Lottie heard him this time but thought she was imagining

the sound of his voice. What was this thing on the floor? Woven corn husks, perhaps. Cloth, a sack that was made of —

"LOTTIE!" Lewis appeared in the doorway. He saw his friend sprawled on the stone floor. He saw the unusual sack near her head. He saw her reach for it.

The NightKing saw Lottie's hand move. "NO!" He dove across the room and their hands slipped deeply into the corn husk sack at the same instant. There was a strange rushing, crackling sound. Lewis flew headfirst across the room toward Lottie and screamed her name once more as he watched her disappear. Lottie felt like she was spilling, being poured from one space into another.

And she wasn't alone.

CHAPTER TWELVE

The Spinning Room

It was deep in the middle of the night back in Oxford, Iowa.

Lottie's eyes took a while to adjust before she knew where she was. There was milky moonlight coming from somewhere. Lottie saw a large window high above her letting in the dim light from behind gauzy curtains. Something large and soft was behind her back. Struggling to her feet and grappling about with her hand, she realized what it was. It was a massive footstool. She was in the Giant Room of her own house.

She and her father had built this room the summer that Lottie turned five. She had read a book about miniature people and wanted to know what it felt like to be the size of a squirrel. Eldon had constructed the towering furniture: a table with two chairs that were twelve feet high, a bookshelf that reached the twenty-foot ceiling and was stacked with giant books they had made together, an enormous beanbag chair that Lottie and Lewis had made and filled with seed corn from —

Seed corn — suddenly Lottie remembered the corn husk sack and realized that it was still in her hand. She didn't understand. Had this brought her back home? If it had, she could use it to rescue Lewis.

Then she heard a moan.

It was a low grumbling moan in the darkness near her left foot. Lottie's insides froze as she realized who it was. She could smell the same strong stale odor that permeated the windmill in LightLand. She could see dark, empty eyes flatly reflecting what little light was in the room. The NightKing had come back to Iowa with her.

Something was wrong with him. His moaning sounded terrible, and it gave Lottie the creeps. She desperately wanted more light. The only lamp in this room, she knew, was connected to a switch ten feet from the floor. There was a rope ladder on the wall to use for reaching it. Lottie didn't want to turn her back on the NightKing.

She tried to pull the corn husk sack closer to herself, but it was stuck. She tugged, and there was a loud moan and sigh. *The NightKing must still be holding on to it,* she thought.

What should she do? She had to move away from him,

but she needed to keep the sack. She needed to bring it back to Lewis. It might be his only way home!

She took a deep breath and pulled the sack with all her might. There was resistance at first and then she had it! She let the momentum of the tug move her, rolling away from the NightKing as quietly as she could. He moaned loudly, but nothing else seemed to happen. Lottie began to inch herself farther away from him. She needed to get help. She had to get out of the Giant Room and reach her father. He would be asleep and would never hear her calling.

Lottie decided to crawl under the huge footstool instead of going around. It was the most direct route to the door, and she felt more protected beneath it. The floor was incredibly soft. She and her father had used remnant carpeting from the 1970s, when ultrashag was the style. The thick beige pile was fully four inches deep. The carpet was very dusty under the footstool, and Lottie felt her nose begin to twitch. She tried to crawl faster, and rubbed her nose frantically, but the feeling grew. And then she sneezed. And sneezed. Seven horrible loud sneezes.

The moaning stopped abruptly. Lottie froze. She heard the NightKing moving. *Bump. Clunk.* He grumbled and stumbled in the dark room. *He doesn't know where he is,* Lottie thought. She silently crawled the rest of the way, holding her breath, afraid of sneezing again. She wanted to call out for her father but knew it was useless. He was a very deep sleeper. She had to get to his door, silently. Lottie didn't think that the NightKing had realized she was there, and she wanted to keep it that way as long as possible.

Ouch. Lottie had bumped into something with her knee — it was her father's enormous Coleman flashlight. He had won it in a raffle years ago and they had been delighted because it was perfect for the Giant Room. They hadn't used it often, because it was terribly heavy and the light was so intense that it gave them a headache.

Lottie secured the corn husk sack carefully around her waist. The rough fabric felt fragile, and she didn't know if it would work again if she ripped it. Then she raised the flashlight with two hands and felt for the On/Off switch. She backed against the wall and had to catch her breath. The excitement made her heart race. She was so afraid that the NightKing would hear her before she was ready that she found herself breathing even louder. His moaning had stopped, and he was starting to move. He was fumbling closer to her. She couldn't let him recover before she had a chance to escape. She would blind him with the intense light.

Lottie stood up and raised the heavy flashlight with some difficulty. She pointed it in the direction of the moaning and she flipped the switch to On.

She hit her target, and the NightKing howled with discomfort in the sudden light. Lottie squinted and could see him flailing around, trying to cover his eyes with his arms. She meant to run, but she hesitated. She stood panting, staring hard at the pathetic man squirming in the glare.

He didn't look like the NightKing. He looked like a confused old man. He looked like Lewis's father. Lottie faltered. She felt a little sorry for him.

That was a mistake.

Truly, the NightKing *was* pathetic at that moment. Returning to Iowa after so many long years in LightLand was agony for him. All that time he had used magic and intimidation to make himself strong and powerful. He had hidden carefully from light. But the majority of his power had evaporated when he touched the inside of the corn husk sack. Now the glare of Lottie's flashlight drowned him in more light than he had suffered through in years. Lottie Cook was breaking him down. But when he saw the beam of light slip and falter, he knew that she was weakening.

"Help me, Lottie," he whispered.

Lottie felt her heart sink. What should she do now? Her hands trembled, and the light bobbled again.

"Lottie," he called feebly. With the strong beam of light bouncing off his eyes, they almost didn't look empty and cold. Almost. What could she do?

"M-Mr. Weaver?" Lottie whispered.

Before she knew what was happening, he lurched toward her, knocking the flashlight from her hands. The bulb inside must have cracked when it fell, because the light was extinguished. In the darkness, Lottie felt as though everything were moving in slow motion. She slipped backward through the door and felt his icy hands trying to stop her. She managed to get away and stumbled down the crooked hall. She called for her father, but there was no answer. She kept running. By instinct, she raced easily up the uneven ramp that raised the floor several inches higher.

Behind her she could hear thuds and grunts as the NightKing fell. He didn't know his way through the maze of the Cooks' house. Lottie, however, knew it like the back of her hand. She tried to ease silently into the Leaf Room. The mulch floor muffled her steps. If he didn't follow her in here, she could disappear through one of the trap doors in the ceiling and make her way to her father.

But then she heard him breathing heavily in the open door. She sprinted across the leaf mulch and dove headfirst into the wall.

She disappeared from the room through a small tunnel hidden in the wall. Even as she vanished, the NightKing gave a roar and raged into the Leaf Room, swooping with his arms, trying to catch Lottie in the darkness.

The dark and the musty smell of the Leaf Room suited the NightKing. He felt better. He stood in the center of the small, crooked room and listened for Lottie.

She was scrambling through the secret passage and quickly came out on the other side into the Spinning Room. It was much brighter because the walls and ceiling and floor were pasted with silvery metallic wallpaper. They reflected moonlight from three windows in the ceiling. Lottie could see herself reflected in a thousand distorted ways.

The floor was a circular stage that turned like a lazy Susan. The curving walls spun on a separate track. Lottie reached back, tugged on a lever inside the passage, and creaking, the walls began to revolve.

Lottie moved to the center of the room and steadied her feet. When the walls spun, the secret passage was open only once in each revolution, as the hole in the wall matched up with the hole in the tunnel. It would be difficult for the NightKing to get in. And nearly impossible for Lottie to get out past him.

In the tunnel, the NightKing still clutched the deadly blue bag he had been holding back in the windmill. His own powers may have weakened, but he felt certain that the magic woven into the fabric would not waver. As the opening spun past the tunnel he could see the many reflections of Lottie Cook flicker before his eyes. He counted the speed in his mind and precisely calculated the exact moment to move.

Lottie made certain that the corn husk sack was securely tied at her waist. She groped for her cherry seed. *Where was it?* Finally she pulled the seed from the hem of her pajamas and clutched it in her fist. She steeled herself for his appearance; she was ready. Still, when he came through the hole it was terrifying.

The NightKing hurtled out of the silvery wall, all boney arms and swirling gray clothes. Lottie flinched, but she did not scream. She saw the blue bag he carried. Was it the Veil of Oblivion? Lottie didn't know. There was no place to hide. There was no way to escape from this room. Getting back out through the secret passage meant clinging to the wall and finding the lever while spinning around. No, the battle would be here. And now.

The NightKing sprawled dizzily on the unsteady floor. Lottie rocked side to side on her feet as though riding a skateboard. The floor shifted heavily with her movements as she threw her weight first one way and then the other. Back and forth, the NightKing was thrown. He stumbled three times as he tried to get to his feet.

Lottie remained standing, swaying in the center of the floor. Her palms were wet, and she could feel the cherry seed in her fist like a stone. She kept her eyes on the top of his head. She knew from experience that when the silvery walls and floor moved at the same time, it was extremely disorienting. If she had looked up she would have lost her balance and probably been sick. Lottie's best chance now, she thought, would be if she could make the NightKing throw up.

He trudged ferociously toward her on all fours, falling when he became lost in the images of Lottie and himself tangled on the spinning walls. Still, he got closer to her. Almost close enough to touch. Lottie slid carefully back. And then she began to run.

She ran in a circle, timing her steps with the turning floor. It was a treadmill. The faster she ran, the faster the floor turned. The NightKing howled and was thrown on his back with the momentum. His blood boiled. He had to destroy Lottie Cook. He had to do it now. He had to get her into his deadly blue bag.

This bag had only been used once, several years before. The results had been so gruesome that even the NightKing had hesitated to use it again. He had made the bag by weaving together the memories of his youngest, most innocent victims with the memories of his most evil rat-servants. The tension in the fabric was intense. The bag itself vibrated all the time, as though it wanted to split itself in two.

He smiled a horrible smile and pulled himself upright on the spinning floor. He would catch Lottie when she ran close to him. He had the deadly bag ready.

But Lottie stopped just in time. She jumped and turned in midair, running in the opposite direction. The floor lurched and reversed, sending the NightKing crashing into the spinning walls. He crumpled into the mirrored edge of a wall panel.

The effect was impressive. Lottie had practiced these moves many times. She had spent hours alone, playing at warfare against imagined villains. But this time the villain was genuine. She no longer felt sorry for him. She no longer worried that he was Lewis's father. He was the NightKing. And she would defeat him. She ran faster, jumped, turned, ran. He fell again. And again. He moaned and turned green.

The NightKing was battered by Lottie's control of the spinning floor. And when he gathered up his strength and tried to pounce at her, he found himself muddled by the reflections. He no longer knew how to unravel the tricks of light. Lottie was winning.

And then she slipped.

Lottie slid with a sickening thud and ended tangled at the NightKing's feet. He raised one black boot and pushed it firmly into her chest, pinning her to the floor.

Lottie looked up into his horrible face and shuddered. "Be still!" he hissed at Lottie Cook. "You've no chance left!"

But Lottie would not be still. She *did* have a chance. She thrashed and kicked and flailed with her fists. She screamed for her father, but the sound bounced back off the mirrored walls. The NightKing grimaced as he restrained her, his boot keeping her pinned down. He tried to open the bag, but Lottie kept batting his arms and knocking the bag aside.

With a howl of rage the NightKing seized her left arm, twisting it hard the wrong way. Lottie didn't scream or cry out. Her thoughts floated across her mind in slow motion. Was she going to faint? That would be the end of her . . . the NightKing would win after all. Her memories would be lost forever. He would start with her cherry tree.

Her cherry tree . . . Something buzzed in Lottie's mind. Back in the windmill, the scared lab mouse had told her something. . . .

Lottie's eyes had glazed over, but now she saw a dark blue hole gaping above her. It was the deadly bag. With her right hand Lottie still clutched the small smooth cherry seed. With her last ounce of strength she threw the seed into the growing darkness.

There was first a small noise, a crackling, popping sound. Little lights seemed to be ricocheting deep within the fabric itself. Startled, the NightKing lowered the bag. Lottie saw his face as he strained to find out what had happened. There was a split second of recognition as the NightKing gaped dumbstruck at Lottie still pinned below him. And then there was an explosion.

From where Lottie lay on the floor, it looked as though the mouth of the bag instantly swelled to ten times its size. She felt herself tumbling, sucked into its blue darkness.

But again, she wasn't alone.

The NightKing was brought against his will this time, sucked in by the deep vacuum that the bag had become. As long as she lived, Lottie never forgot the look of horror on his face.

When Lottie had tossed her cherry seed into the open bag everything had changed. She didn't understand it until much later. The bag had been woven for an evil purpose. It possessed a desperate hunger for all things evil and dark. The cherry seed, however, was a concentrated, distilled form of the purest, happiest sort of memory. It was innocent and it was good. And it disturbed the fabric of the bag down to its very molecules.

Lottie never told what she saw inside that bag. She only said that she didn't remember or couldn't be sure. That may not have been quite true. Lottie didn't *want* to remember and didn't *want* to be sure.

The spinning of the room faded in her mind as she spun through the darkness of the bag with greater speed than she could ever have imagined. A horrible, howling scream filled the air. At first Lottie thought that she was screaming, but then she realized that, while her mouth was thrown wide open, the howling came from outside herself.

There was a sour, acidic smell that was almost unbearable. She'd have stopped breathing to avoid it if she knew how. The force of the spinning was so strong it held her eyes and mouth wide open. She couldn't see the NightKing, but he had to be the one screaming.

And then suddenly, everything stopped.

Lottie felt herself tumble to earth. The screaming was gone. The smell had vanished. She was surrounded by blinding light. Lottie felt a terrible dryness in her mouth and eyes as she closed them. There was suddenly pain in her left arm.

If it hurts, I must be alive, she thought. And then she knew no more.

CHAPTER THIRTEEN

Fireflies

When Lottie and the NightKing had both grasped the corn husk sack and vanished from LightLand, Lewis had collapsed in the grim room at the center of the windmill fortress. He pounded the stone of the floor where they had disappeared.

October Mouse said nothing. The Veil of Oblivion had been secreted away safely. That had been their mission. But had it cost Lewis his Lottie Cook? And without her, could they be strong enough to fight the NightKing when he returned, as surely he would?

A long time went by. The voices that always filled the air inside the windmill seemed to grow louder. The fortress continued to shake and rumble. The mouse felt certain it would collapse on top of them, but he would not disturb his friend in his despair.

Finally Lewis stood. The mouse scrambled up his leg and climbed into his pocket. Lewis walked methodically through the corridors and down the unsteady stone steps. He saw no sign of anyone. The stones quivered under his feet. At one point, as they passed through an archway, the room just behind them imploded with a crash of dust and flying rock. October trembled and hid his face, but Lewis didn't even seem to notice.

When they finally stepped out of the fortress, the air outside revived them both. It was cold and clean. It smelled green, like things growing. A steady wind blew, but the windmill blades didn't move. The unsettling of the foundation must have jammed them. Already, they looked crooked and bent. Lewis walked back out across the stones that were etched deeply in the cryptic marks like the ones in his notebook. He grimaced as he stepped on them.

It was the end of the day. The sun was slipping away to the west. This was the time when all good creatures in LightLand fled below ground to find safety for the night. October shivered and worried. His friend Lewis was not going to hide ever again, October felt sure of it.

A bird called high above them. Sent by Umber, no doubt, it was a large crow. CoalBlack Crow, October recognized her. The bird circled and seemed to be signaling, but didn't come close. As Lewis and October looked up at the late afternoon sky, there was a great roar.

The windmill moved. It shook and shimmered in the twilight. Then it collapsed. The deafening sound of those massive stones crashing down pounded against Lewis's eardrums, and he stumbled backward. When it was all still again, the pile of dust and pebbles looked like the relics in the Weavers' backyard in Iowa. And it was silent. The voices were gone.

Lewis gaped. He stood and blinked, unable to believe his eyes.

CoalBlack Crow circled one last time and then flew off. She would report this news to Robert and Umber. Finally Lewis turned and stumbled away. October rode silently in his pocket.

Lewis was numb. He just walked. He came to the massive cornfield and kept walking through it. And then he saw a tree far in the distance. He didn't stop, but a small smile crossed his face.

Lewis walked and walked as if he were walking home. The corn still smelled sweet to him, although it was turning dry and brown. Fallen stalks crunched under his feet. He had to push the slanted stalks out of his way with each step. When he came out on the other side, the sun was truly setting. The yellow light was suddenly hot and intense in his face. The only thing breaking up the strong rays was Lottie's cherry tree, straight ahead. Lewis felt his pulse race and walked steadily to it.

When he arrived he knew for certain why he'd been walking. Because, there in the clover under the tree, not sleeping and not awake either, was Lottie.

The light of the setting sun beat down on her through the branches. Her favorite lavender pajamas were filthy. The hem was ripped loose. Her face was cut and dirty. Lewis had never been so glad to see someone in his life.

It took a while to get Lottie to answer him. She was in a daze. She didn't understand that she was back in LightLand. When he touched her arm she whimpered in pain. Lewis still had the yellow cloth hanging from his pocket. He pulled the fabric apart at the seams. It tore easily into a long smooth piece. Without a word, Lewis fashioned a sling and eased Lottie's arm into it. Lottie's eyelids fluttered, and she realized that she was back with Lewis. She was too weak to talk.

He helped her sit up, propped against her tree. She faded in and out of awareness. As Lewis tried to make her comfortable, he felt a hard something twisted up in Lottie's polar fleece pocket. He untwisted it and was startled when his own notebook tumbled out onto the cold ground.

It had changed. Something magical had happened. The

cover had turned the color of pure silver. Lewis kneeled and opened the small book. The symbols were gone. Where there had been squiggles and sketchy marks, there were now words. Words in his own handwriting. It was a story. It was, Lewis realized with a gasp, the story of everything he knew. He had been writing it all along. He sat in stunned silence, reading the story that he had not known he was writing. The story he had never heard before and yet knew by heart all the same.

October Mouse gently slid to the ground. The thoughtful creature did not disturb either Lottie or Lewis, who were both lost in their own worlds. That brave mouse would have fought to the bitter end anyone who dared try to disturb the two children.

Suddenly something flew past October's face. A glowing, humming spark of light. A firefly. It was twilight. The stars were just beginning to come out. October had never seen the night sky. The mouse gasped at the sight of the first star he had ever seen — glimmering up there in the velvety blue-blackness. *How beautiful!* October turned to look at the other half of the endless sky, and there, above the top of the rubble of the windmill, the full moon glowed. It looked just exactly like a bowl of custard. . . .

Lottie wavered in the gathering darkness between knowing where she was and having absolutely no idea. She felt as though she were floating along in the easy quiet of the evening. The battle was over. She didn't really know how it had turned out. But she had done her best. That feeling gave her great peace of mind for the first time in days and days. She floated on it.

Lottie soon realized that she wasn't dying. Or even dreaming. Lewis stayed by her side, holding his transformed journal. Something gnawed at Lottie's mind.

"Lewis?" she whispered.

"Yes?"

"He came after me . . . back to Iowa."

Lewis nodded. "I thought so," he said.

"Lewis?" Lottie whispered and felt her throat closing up.

"Yes?"

"I don't know where he is. . . . He might be dead. Or he might not."

Lewis just nodded. It would matter a great deal, one way or the other, whether his father was still alive. But they would have to face that another night. Not this night.

As the evening gave way to real darkness, something else happened. The silence gave way as well.

At first it was an owl. (The same owl, actually, who had noticed Lewis that first night that he entered LightLand.) "*Who . . . Whooooo!*" And then a nightingale's song, so pretty that it made October ache with love for it. And then other noises that the night in LightLand had not known in years.

There were voices. And even someone singing.

Lottie and Lewis squinted to see. Robert was coming. He carried a torch and led a small group of the citizens of LightLand. Weary and wide-eyed, they seemed not to believe what they saw. *Who are they?* Lottie wanted to know. *Are they out of hiding from NightRooms below ground? Are they more victims of the NightKing and his Veil?*

The torches were sunk into the ground and others were hastily fashioned out of cornstalks by Robert and Lewis to make a wide glowing circle around the tree. Robert kept wandering from the light of the circle to see the night sky more clearly. Then he came to the center to speak, and his voice was clear and calm.

"My friends," he said, looking in turn at Lottie, Lewis, October, and Umber. "I feel as though I have returned from a long voyage. I have back every moment of my life. Every memory, every story, every precious thing . . ."

Lottie could hardly believe that this was the same boy she had seen mumble in his sleep that first time in the NightRoom.

"Now all of LightLand is ours again. Not only its sunlit days, but also its sparkling nights! And we are strong and whole again." As Robert spoke, Lewis noticed that the crowd below the tree was growing. There were people coming from all directions. He saw a yellow-haired woman with tears in her eyes slip into the circle next to him. The woman watched Robert speak and her face glowed with pride.

"We celebrate tonight, but we must also swear to be watchful. Never again can we let a tyrant divide us by stealing our greatest strengths." The crowd cheered and someone called out, "Is he dead? Is he truly gone?"

All eyes turned toward Lottie and Lewis. Lewis shook his head, raising his eyebrows. Lottie looked downward and shrugged. They simply didn't know.

The residents of LightLand were frightened.

"The Veil! Where is the Veil?!"

"Has it really been destroyed?"

Robert stepped back and gestured toward the tree. There in the branches, a red flame shimmered. The Veil of Oblivion hung from the cherry tree, its ends streaming in the wind. A hush fell over the crowd. And then the quiet broke with a loud roar of voices. They were afraid.

"Quiet, friends," Robert called. "Peace!" As the crowd quieted, Umber made his way to Robert's shoulder. "We do not know how to destroy the Veil, but I believe that only Lewis can be charged with removing it from LightLand."

The crowd turned its eyes on Lewis again. "Yes," he

answered in a clear voice. "The NightKing was my father. But I am no longer his son."

Lottie's eyes widened as she watched Lewis speak to the crowd. Not only was he *speaking,* he was . . . brave.

It was true, of course. Lewis had never before thought of himself as the brave one. That was Lottie. But in LightLand he had stood alone, face-to-face with the NightKing. At that moment Lewis had realized that he was braver and stronger than anyone would have imagined.

"If I can find my way out of LightLand," Lewis continued, "I will carry the Veil away with me."

The crowd was divided. Some cheered Lewis, and others chattered nervously, "If he can? What does he mean, *if* he can?"

Lottie walked over to be next to her friend. There was something in her hand. "I have the way home, Lewis."

It was the corn husk sack.

Lewis unwrapped the yellow bandage strip and used it to pick up the flaming fabric of the Veil. Lottie touched the same yellow flannel that was binding her arm. With surprise she realized it was no longer throbbing. The soft yellow sling comforted her. "I don't want to take my sling off yet," she said.

"No, that's all right," said Lewis. "Mine is enough."

Lewis held his unwrapped hand up for the mouse to see. October was delighted and bobbed up and down. Lewis's hand looked as good as new. If you examined it very, very closely, there was only the thinnest of scars.

Carefully, Lewis folded the red shimmering Veil of Oblivion into the smallest possible bundle. It still made his fingers tingle and tremble, but it was not the same as it had been before. It didn't affect his mind. Lewis tied it securely with the soft yellow strip of cloth. October helped as Lewis wrapped the yellow flannel around and around until no red showed through at all.

Umber couldn't help shuddering as Lewis slipped the wrapped bundle inside his shirt. The bird had suffered enough just holding the hated thing in his three-toed claw. Nothing could make him put it near to his heart like that. But Lewis didn't mind. Actually it made him feel stronger.

It was now time to go home. Lottie carefully spread the corn husk sack on the ground, and then they all gasped. The sack was torn.

Down at the bottom, there was a fist-size hole, almost as though a bite had been taken from it.

Lottie trembled as she remembered. "At home, in the Giant Room . . . the NightKing had a hold of the sack, too. I tugged it away from him, but he must have ripped it. Will it still work?" she asked.

"Yes," Lewis answered so definitively that they were all surprised. He knelt down, hunching over, tugging on the corn husks. He twisted and tied. By the time he sat up, the sack was whole again. The bottom had a wave to it, like the top of a cornfield — straight, but not quite straight.

They all nodded at one another and then, without needing to say good-bye, Lottie and Lewis slipped their arms into the sack. They thought that they heard Zerox howl.

And then LightLand was gone.

But not forgotten.

CHAPTER FOURTEEN

"Everything i Know"

When Mr. Cook and Ms. d'Avignon finally woke Lottie and Lewis, days had gone by.

It wasn't until Saturday morning that Lewis had appeared, sound asleep with his face buried under a pillow, on the living room sofa. Worried, Eldon searched the house for Lottie. Finally he pulled himself into the tunnel that led to the spinning room.

Or what used to be the spinning room. The ceiling, floor, and walls had melted and burned and cooled again into a dark, glassy surface, like the inside of a seashell. And there in the center was Lottie. Asleep, banged up, dirty, her arm tied in the yellow sling. But she was home. Tucked under her good arm was the StoryBox.

She opened her eyes with a snap when he touched the

StoryBox. She saw her father and her teacher kneeling over her. The first word out of her mouth was —

"Lewis?"

They nodded, and Lottie ran to wake him. He sat bolt upright, blinking and smiling.

"Thank you," he said out loud. Lottie beamed. Lewis felt in his shirt for the Veil. It was still there. But, they realized later, neither of them had the sack made of corn husks that had brought them home. Had it disintegrated?

Eldon and Margo made tea and corn biscuits and heard the story of the liberation of LightLand. Lottie stood on the couch and told the tale with grand hand gestures and reenactments.

Lewis spoke too, and wasn't the least bit self-conscious. Mr. Cook and Ms. d'Avignon beamed at him. He interjected the parts that he had gone through alone. Lottie couldn't help noticing that he seemed much older when he spoke of his father.

Neither of them told what Lewis carried bundled in his shirt. It seemed to them that it was too great a secret to share. The fewer people that knew, the better. After all, if the NightKing was still out there somewhere, with a handful of magically woven corn husks, he might someday try to find his treasured Veil of Oblivion.

It was getting late. When the telephone rang, they all knew it would be Lucille Weaver, home from Peoria and looking for her son. With a mischievous smile, Lewis himself answered the phone. "Hello, this is Lewis speaking," he said. For once, the silence was on the other end of the phone.

Lottie couldn't control her laughter as Lewis tried to get his mother to respond. "Mother? Is that you?" he asked over and over. All he could hear was a faint spluttering sound. "I'll be right home," he told her, hanging up the phone. As Lewis left to make sure his mother hadn't had some kind of nervous attack, he silently thumped his chest where the bundle was still hidden. Lottie only nodded slightly so the adults wouldn't notice, and they all said good night.

The next day Lewis cheerfully said, "Good morning!" to Betsy Pelican. It took Betsy a second to realize what had happened, and then she tripped and fell right into the post office hedge.

He startled people all over school. The only person who didn't seem surprised when he spoke was Alice Atwell. Alice looked extremely pleased. Lottie and Lewis were having a great day.

Then it was time for P.E. Coach Haggler rubbed his hands as they filed in. "Starting today," he announced, "all sixth graders are going to have weekly P.E. tests. Any questions?" He spoke slowly and stared at Lottie, daring her to raise her hand. "No? No one has anything to say? I need a volunteer to show how it's done," he stroked his double chin. "Oh, I don't know, how about . . . Lottie Cook." The coach walked to his office doorway where he'd mounted a chin-up bar. He blew his whistle. "Thirty chin-ups!"

The class murmured.

"You don't want to fail, do you?" Coach Haggler turned his back to demonstrate. He was strong. He did thirty in no time. He did ten more with just his right arm. "Nobody has any questions. Nobody has anything to say, so —"

"*I* have something to say."

It was a voice Coach Haggler had never heard before. "Yeah," he growled, finishing his chin-ups and turning around. "Yeah, who has something to say to me?"

"I do."

It was Lewis. Coach Haggler turned purple. He thought he was being mocked. Somebody was tricking him — that wimpy Weaver kid couldn't talk!

Lewis stood up and spoke calmly. "She has a broken arm. You can't make her do anything. Besides, we never did chin-ups before and it's not fair. If you're failing Lottie, then you'll have to fail me, too."

"And me."

Shy Alice Atwell was on her feet.

"Me, too!" It was Betsy Pelican. Pretty soon the whole class was standing. (Brian Goode and Alan Wolf just sat and stared.) Coach Haggler was ready to explode.

"Who's the coach here?!" he spluttered furiously. "I am! You stupid kids don't get to decide ANYTHING." With that he slammed his way through the gym doors and stormed down the hall toward the office.

The class cheered. They played a friendly game of touch football until the buzzer buzzed. They didn't see the coach for the rest of the day.

That afternoon Mr. Cook wanted Lottie's arm examined. Dr. Lee was amazed by the injury. It seemed to have been broken all right, in two places. But somehow it had already healed. An X ray revealed two tidy mends in the bone. Lottie shrugged and looked innocent as she clutched the soft yellow sling protectively.

Lottie and Lewis left for school early on Tuesday morning. They needed time to talk privately. They walked slowly through the cornfield. Lewis's shirt still bulged over his heart where he carried the Veil. "I'm afraid to leave it at home," he explained.

Lottie agreed. What if Mrs. Weaver found it and unwrapped it? "But I sure don't want to carry it around for the rest of my life either," Lewis added.

225

In the end they devised a very good plan. They managed to sneak out of their houses late that night. From her father's Building Room, Lottie brought his largest auger. They drilled a deep hole in the smooth flat stump of Lottie's cherry tree. Lewis solemnly unwound the soft yellow bundle with his bare hands. He refused the gloves that Lottie had brought for his protection. The smoldering red Veil of Oblivion shimmered and flashed just as brightly in their own world. They knew that it was still potent and dangerous. It crackled and stung Lewis's hands. He flinched but did not drop it.

Lewis packed the Veil into the tree stump and then filled the hole with a paste they made using the sawdust from the auger mixed with shellac and corn syrup. It was a mess, but hardened quickly and nearly invisibly.

The strips of yellow flannel were another matter. They didn't *seem* dangerous. (Although, since they had been woven by the NightKing, one could never be exactly sure of what they might do.) Lottie and Lewis found that they each felt strangely attached to their respective bits.

They decided that they would keep them. Lottie kept hers inside her StoryBox. Lewis kept his under his pillow.

Ms. d'Avignon collected first drafts of their essays the next week. The sixth graders had done a pretty good job. At least, they had tried. After all, most people never bother to wonder or to find out how very much they know. Or to test the limits of what they can do. The vast majority of people, it seems, stumble along using a tenth of their brain and their power and the modest magic that is deep inside them all along.

Lottie and Lewis were among the exceptions. They knew everything that they knew.

Before school was let out for Columbus Day, they had to submit their final essays to Ms. d'Avignon. Lewis had written his life story. It was seventy-three pages long.

Here is Lottie's essay. It wasn't terribly long, but she could not have written it during her lunch hour.

"Everything I Know" by Charlotte Cook

There are two kinds of things that I know. The first are the things that I have *learned.* Those are easy to tell you about. . . .

I have learned how to cook and how to build an extra room onto my house. I know how to start a fire (ask permission first) and when to rake the leaves. I know how to curry a horse and how to milk a cow and how to trim a rabbit's toenails (very carefully). I know how to jump rope (hot pepper) and ice-skate (dry your blades) and cut hair (two styles). I know how to whistle every song I ever heard. I know all the verses to "Amazing Grace." I know how to make a wreath out of grapevines and how to get a scrape to stop bleeding (with moss). I know how to make my bed so that you could bounce a nickel on it (even if I don't do that very often). I know where my father hides my Christmas presents in the barn.

I know which way is north. I can read a map. I know when it's going to snow (you can *smell* it). I know that a good book is fun to read twice (at least). I know where babies come from (ask your aunt). I know a little history, a little geography and civics, some arithmetic (they force it on you). I know some things about science. I know what a rainbow would look like if I could see it from above (that's physics). I know how to find the Big Dipper and the Little Dipper and especially my favorite, Orion's Belt (which I'd like to try on for size someday). I know what I like (pepper jelly). I know what I don't (dodgeball). I know who my friends are.

I have learned that there is such a thing as real magic. I don't always know where to find it, but I do know enough to look.

The other things I know are some things that it seems like I've *always* known or always had inside me.

Some of these things are harder to describe. For instance, I have always known that I am different from most people. It's hard to say why. My family is different, and my memory is different, too.

People have looked at me funny my entire life. Sometimes sad, sometimes curious. They say stuff about my mother, like, "Wouldn't your mother be proud?" Or else, "Now what would your mother say?"

I've always shrugged. Those kinds of questions were things that I just didn't know how to answer. But now I do.

I found out recently what I should have known my whole life. I found out that I am carrying my mother around inside me. She is right here. Right along with all of my other memories. Memory runs deep. Deeper than one lifetime or two. Deeper than time, if you'll let it. This is also one of the things that I know.

I know that I can do anything. If I need to do something badly enough, and if I really concentrate on it hard enough, I can do it. Whatever it is. Even if it is impossible.

I know what's important. I know what isn't. At least for now. I know that all we have is what we can remember.

ACKNOWLEDGMENTS

One night I called my grandfather to tell him some good news. He had already taken off his hearing aid and he barked, "I can't hear a word you're saying, but I sure am proud of you." This is the kind of support that my family has always given me.

Thank you, first readers: Nardi Reeder Campion, George Singer, Matthew Hedley, Sarah Robson, Miriam and Melanie Subbiah, Margo Doscher's class in Norwich, Vermont (who said, "We like it because it could really happen") and the good listeners at John Lyman School in Middlefield, Connecticut.

Thank you, Charles Melcher, President of Melcher Media and talented friend, who steered me in the right direction every time. Thank you Amy Griffin, skillful editor at Orchard Books, and Jean Feiwel at Scholastic.

Thank you, inspirations: Aunt Lottie Cook. Julia, Hugh, Alan, Audrey, and Scott McCutchen.

Our daughters, Julia and Catherine. And my husband, Thomas Kannam, from the first chapter to the last.